THE PELEG

FOUNDLINGS

CHRONICLES

Matthew Christian Harding

www.MatthewChristianHarding.com

FOUNDLINGS

Zoe and Sozo Publishing
3034 Millers Landing Rd.
Gloucester, Virginia 23061

www.MatthewChristianHarding.com

Cover Design by Zoe and Sozo Publishing

All scripture references are from the King James Version of the Bible.

ISBN 978-0-9823484-0-6

Praise for *The Peleg Chronicles*

Blue Ribbon Award for Best Book 2010-2011
— The Old Schoolhouse Magazine

"Like gnarled roots of an old tree, these stories twist and turn, entangling you in anticipation to see how they all unwind …
The story follows the heroic adventures of a handful of God-fearing men and children. These often funny and endearing characters show us what can be accomplished when you learn to overcome your fears and walk in faith …
The books read like fantasy novels, yet without magic spells, wands, and flying broomsticks. Instead, Scripture and prayer are revealed as the powerful tools needed to overcome the works of those who obey the evil one; to offer hope to our heroes in desperate times; and to give them boldness to share their faith along the way. God's redemptive power is also plainly evident when even a sworn enemy can turn to the one true God …
A thrilling cliffhanger ends each story so be sure to read them in order. I can't wait to find out what happens in the next one.
Maybe these "magic-free" character-building, God-honoring novels will start a new trend … I hope so!"
— Nigel Andreola, *Christian Book Distributors*

"Great book! I would like the book to be about 500 pages; no, 600 pages. The doctrines and examples are powerful. Can you do a new series about the Giants? Maybe a short story? How about Fergus' training from a youth? Thiery's memorization days with Oded? Back story, side story, or continuing story! Maybe even a short play by Gettlefinger? Your stories are a delight to my family. Your messages strengthen our faith. Your doctrines strengthen our resolve to live by God's word alone. Sola Scriptura. May God be praised!"
— Peter Rowell, father of five

"I asked my daughter what she like so much about this book and she said "because there's no blank space. I mean, there's not any space where nothing's happening. There's always something important happening". I have read it and can say the same thing. There is excitement with every sentence. You won't want to put the book down, and when you come to the end ... you're going to want more! It's refreshing to read such a wonderful book."
— **Mona Lisa,** *www.happilyhomeschooling.com*

"I believe this series is the answer to many parent's prayers."
— **Lauren,** *mother of 4*

"I completely and utterly love this book! ... I loved everything about the book, especially Horatio. I can't wait for more!"
— **Courtney,** *age 16*

"This book gets not only approval but a standing ovation. Do not be mistaken and think this book will also be devoid of adventure, thrills, fun and challenging thoughts. Foundlings not only gives you a ride that combats any roller coaster it gives you a true sense of heroism and family discussions that center on the glory of God's creation and Word. Think your kid is not interested in the Bible or Christian books? This book will change both your minds."
— **Richele,** *Under the Golden Apple Tree*

"It is refreshing to be entertained by a story that has faith in God as its centerpiece. Matthew Harding, in his book *Foundlings*, portrays a fantasy epic that is both compelling and God-honoring. Several characters are drawn to the hope and promises of our Creator as they deal with the internal struggles of their own human nature and observe the hope, grace and love from the followers of the one true God. The tale entertains, uplifts and inspires readers of all ages. But most importantly, it fosters a biblical worldview and godly character into the hearts and minds of our youth."
— **Jeff Purkiss,** Founder, *Squires2Knights Ministries*

For my Princepessa,

My wife, my help meet, my best friend

Table Of Contents

—The Gospel—

Staffsmitten's map

Prologue

"There be dragons. There be giants. And God: our maker, our help, and our righteous judge." The warrior's broad hand rested upon the eager shoulder of a boy. "Does it not stir your soul?"

It was in the days of Peleg, when the world was divided. After the flood of Noah, after the tower of Babel and the dispersion, when men wondered where they were upon the earth, and where their fellows had gone to, when beasts were more numerous than men—predators in the wood, in the water, and in the air. But men struggled and fought, carving their place. And in the process of time they once again began to multiply upon the face of the earth.

Lord McDougal

No longer did men call him "The Friendly" or "The Just."

The Witch Esla stood upon the dais, bent beneath her robes, and prophesied a curse over Lord McDougal. "Before the birthing of the sun at year's end, you and yours shall die."

A murmur bubbled and spewed from her prophetic cauldron. The burps and hisses of it could be heard whispering behind closed doors and settling upon the itching ears of the court, then flowing over into the town, and soon it spread throughout his lands.

In just a few days, men would not look him in the eye.

He became Lord McDougal, "The Dead."

His brother had already fallen, a sad but noble tale; then both parents followed from the bloody cough of the white-death. So it was that his people were predisposed to believe the curse.

Still, his brother and parents had died years before.

But then, one week after the Witch had spoken, his younger sisters and guardian were killed by a dragon, and of all places, it happened in the castle garden.

A fortnight later his favorite cousin and uncle were ambushed by giants.

They were all dead. The curse took hold in the minds of men. They felt sure he was next, and none would dare stand with him. That is, none but one.

Then the giants came.

McDougal stood seven feet, eight and three quarter inches, lean and gangly. His legs and arms were unnaturally long, though corded with muscle, and his red hair refused to lay flat upon his head, which bobbed atop an elongated neck. He could not stop himself, and for certain he did not want to stop his boyish face from smiling. But with his members, uncontrolled in most particulars, most knew him as a hobbledy-hoy. Again and again he tried harnessing his body to a more noble presentation as he moved through the space before him. Again and again he would fail.

McDougal placed his legs first one way and then another. His arms swung like elephant trunks as he swiveled his torso in concert to their swaying. So practicing, he held his head up and back, slightly cocked to one side. Then, as if thinking that too unnatural he allowed his head to rock. A slight nausea must have been the result, for his face began to turn a whitish hue and he gagged, and so he changed his gait altogether, self consciously stealing a glance at the man walking beside him.

Accustomed to his master's peculiarities, Fergus Leatherhead gave a slight nod of encouragement. "If you don't mind me saying so sir, the walk you practiced yesterday fit you nicely."

"Was this a bit overdone, then?"

"Yes, sir."

They continued in silence for a time. Fergus repeatedly looked away, embarrassed for his lord.

But then, as it occasionally happened, the lanky arms and legs of McDougal met in a reunion of harmony. It was as if his extremities, true kinsmen, suddenly realized they'd been dining in the same hall all through dinner, and just now as dessert was served, recognized each other and came together in fellowship.

Fergus held his breath, hopeful, but unsure. The unity not only continued, but the kinsmen bond grew so strong, that McDougal seemed as one person again. And Fergus relaxed. Yet to look upon McDougal's oval face, there appeared a frown.

"You have quite found it, sir, a manly stride." But the frown did not dissipate, and now his eyebrows sunk low upon a darkening countenance.

Step after beautiful step they trod through the high grasses of the plateau. While McDougal's thoughts were in a far distant place, Fergus Leatherhead admired the transformation that was occurring.

After all this time, he still marveled at the process: his master could be so awkward and clumsy, and then suddenly embody perfect grace. It seemed to Fergus that McDougal's peculiar problem was that of consuming self study. But then, when his intense cogitations turned to some outward concern or danger, especially a noble enterprise, McDougal became the greatest warrior he had ever known—truly a hero. And while his appearance and carriage often failed the strict standards of the day for a warrior lord, his character and love of the true God set him apart as one worthy to follow.

"I'm looking towards our future, Fergus, and I'm troubled on a few points." McDougal paused, and stared hard at his servant.

Fergus shifted uncomfortably and met his eyes. All his life he had been raised to serve, give counsel, and fight alongside this man. His attentions had focused on McDougal, and he did not like it when notice was unduly focused upon himself, especially if it were of a sentimental nature. And McDougal was decidedly sentimental.

"Let me speak plainly ... I'm wondering if you could help me see my way more clearly ... more plain like, you see."

"Yes, sir." Fergus would try. But just as McDougal had difficulty executing bodily motion, so his words sometimes tumbled and soared in a confusing mixture of what was said, and more importantly what was unsaid, so that it often taxed Fergus to appear as if he understood his master's manner of speaking.

And now Fergus had the added difficulty of steering the conversation away from himself. If possible, he wanted to leave it altogether—to fall away into the grass at their feet, tromped upon, and not worth revisiting.

"These are quite the troublesome circumstances, yes?" McDougal asked.

"Yes, sir."

"It's not as if I have met more misfortune than Job. He lost a lot more than I. This is obvious."

"Yes, sir, obvious."

"Naked came I out of the womb, and naked shall I return and all that, so it's not that I'm grieving on that score, worldly possessions and all. And one day, I'll be rejoined with my family, so, that ache in my heart I know will lessen in time." Here he paused, and then spoke slow and deliberate. "Everything is gone ... Everything but you."

"Yes, sir, I quite see your point."

McDougal's kind eyes curved at their corners. He smiled.

Fergus looked away. McDougal was baring his soul again, and it was clear now he would say something affectionate. Shouldn't a lord be reserved and thereby dignified? Fergus thought so. This was a weakness he had difficulty accepting. Sometimes while listening to or telling a poignant tale, tears would fill McDougal's eyes—tears! At least they were quiet tears: he did not blubber.

But then there was his ear-to-ear grin, which gave one the impression of stupidity, and occasionally he would chuckle, which in his case, furthered the impression—bordering on idiocy.

But worst of all was his laughter, pleasant at first; it threatened all too often a high, piercing, almost screaming howl. His face flushed red, his head thrown back—what to Fergus looked painful—and then between the screaming bellows he would gasp for air, only to repeat the ordeal again.

At best, it was inconsistent and eccentric behavior for the reputation of a lord. At worst: a doltish, and dull-witted reproach upon his position.

Fergus felt his greatest service to his master was to discourage these public displays by any means he could. And so now, he turned stiffly away—a necessary discourtesy—for the developing of his master's deportment.

McDougal slapped Fergus on the back. "You don't know how much of a relief it is to hear you say that. I'm glad we've a new understanding, then."

Fergus swung around to face him. McDougal was beaming with childish abandon, a great invisible burden gone, and Fergus stammered forth his question. "A relief, sir?"

"Well, yes, seeing we grew up together from childhood ... you see."

"We did, sir. Your family has always been good to mine."

"That's just it. Our family condescended as it were. Something I've been ... uneasy with."

"Oh...." This was far from the sentimental praises he had expected. Did he really mean that the McDougal's had lowered themselves too far when they enlisted his own family—that could not be. But what then?

Again he slapped his back and smiled triumphantly. "And so you're now relieved of your duties."

Fergus gasped. "But —"

McDougal's smile disappeared. "What's wrong?"

"You took me by surprise, sir, my oath to you and yours was only to terminate at my death, I never expected it would end this way, to be frank, in disgrace."

McDougal took a step back.

"I am sorry, sir," Fergus said, "that you find my presence too great a condescension. Shall we part now, or in the interest of mutual safety shall we travel together until other arrangements can be made." He proposed this practical remedy to mask his inner turmoil, for Fergus was always practical.

McDougal's mouth hung open. A confused, pained expression shadowed his features—a look that Fergus could not bear—for he had caused it.

Maybe Fergus had not quite understood, and so both men stopped walking and fidgeted. McDougal, mouth agape, began to speak, stopped, tried again, thought better of it, and so on, until he resembled a hatchling at feeding—making tiny unintelligible noises.

It was too much to see his master so incoherently muddled. Giving him a chance to recover, Fergus turned and looked down the slight grade, peppered with occasional outcrops of rock, across a bog cut through by a slithering stream, and into the woods a few hundred feet away.

Then he heard it. It was smashing through under-brush, heading their way, interspersed with moments of pounding feet, then again an explosion of branches and leaves as something snorted—or was it a snarl—in any event it came on, sounding large.

Lyftfloga

The impending encounter would end their discussion and leave an obscuring mist over their friendship, begging a fresh wind of opportunity to raise the mist from their eyes. But for now, years of training and discipline would once again assert McDougal as leader and Fergus as faithful follower.

Fergus glanced at McDougal's excited face—there would be no hesitation or blunders now. When most men grew tense or apprehensive, McDougal would radiate skill and decisive genius. These were Fergus's greatest moments, because they were McDougal's.

"God, You are my God, my soul thirsts for You." More crashing from the woods, and McDougal's voice was clear and strong. "To see your power and glory, what great creature of yours bounds among those trees? Give us wisdom to fight or flee. Strengthen our arms and our hearts."

Between them and the unidentified danger was a great defense—bog and stream. Furthermore they held the high ground, a position not easily approached, and it allowed a commanding view. McDougal held three arrows at the ready; one was nocked upon the string, and a second and third dangled between the fingers of his grip hand. They were Bodkin arrows, having long metal tips which could pierce plate armor at close range. In the arms of a skilled archer, a long bow could shoot a dozen arrows per minute, with accuracy up to two hundred yards. McDougal's first three shots could be fired in a matter of seconds.

Fergus was shield-bearer, sworn protector of his liege lord. Armed with spear and sword, his purpose, he knew, was to defend his master, anticipate danger, and support assault. But keeping up with McDougal's long legs was difficult, and he trembled with excitement about what might come next.

A human voice screaming.

McDougal exploded down the hillside. A moment later, he leapt upon a rock twenty feet from the bog's discernible edge and drew back the first arrow. Fergus scrambled up beside him.

On the other side of the marsh, a man of dwarf height, thickset and slightly hunched, staggered from the woods—a mace outstretched above his head. He peered into the high branches of the forest. But the pursuing creature, whatever it was, did not emerge from the canopy above. Down at the forest floor, near the base of a great dead tree, a black mouth, imbued with yellowed teeth, hissed and snarled. The dwarf screamed and swung his mace through the air, evidently startled by its unexpected position.

The reptilian head was followed by a long winged body. It stalked forward. The man took a step backwards. A step closer to the marsh behind him—bog fattened with quagmires that could slowly absorb his life, any life, into its maw of putrid mud and decay.

The bog, which Fergus had looked upon as a great defense, was no such thing against winged dragon-kind, and furthermore it was a barrier to their assisting the dwarf trapped upon the other side. If the dragon would only move, or open its wings, then McDougal could at least wound the creature.

As the dwarf retreated, closing himself in yet further, a shadowy figure issued forth from just above the tree tops—another dragon. They were Lyftfloga: man-sized, but fierce beasts which frequently worked in pairs to catch their victims. But if horses were about, there could be many more. Lyftfloga could detect a horse from miles away and be worked into a frenzy by the smell and arrival of additional dragons competing for their preferred meal.

Fergus knew it would dive upon its prey. Whichever way the dwarf turned, he would open himself up for an attack from the other. The dwarf had little chance without help.

There was a twang of McDougal's bow. The dragon in flight began its descent.

Another twang. The dragon veered towards the woods, at least one arrow visible in its leathery wing.

Again an arrow sped towards its mark, and the dragon sheered hard against the great dead tree. There was a loud crack, and the tree's dry fibers split as it leaned heavily against a neighboring branch. Its fall seemed imminent.

The dragon was gone.

Taking advantage of the tree top cacophony and the resulting distraction of the dragon before him, the dwarf turned and fled across the bog. In any event, he tried.

McDougal handed Fergus his bow and arrows. "Try to keep 'em off me. But don't cross until I've made a way."

Grabbing Fergus's spear, McDougal ran with great bounding strides, and skimmed himself across the bog, like a child throwing a rock sidearm along the surface of a pond. One, two, three, four, and then five steps, all the way up to the little stream in its center, before McDougal's foot would not rise again.

Coming from the other direction, the poor dwarf attempted a similar feat, his first step landing upon sod that held his weight, and even his second step found relatively solid ground, but fear of the snarling creature at his back, and his short legs, concerted in a terrible misstep that embedded both his feet fast in the mire. Worse yet, trying to turn and face the dragon only caused him to sink at an accelerated pace—any movement at all multiplied the strength and speed of its suck. And so the over-nervous strain stupefied the dwarf into a whimpering, sinking, statue. Almost a statue, for he moved not a limb, but his body quaked silently, and his eyes darted.

McDougal's body continued to move past his mired foot. Falling, he thrust the spear into the muck. With his head down and pressing upon the shaft, the momentum dislodged his feet, and he flipped his body from its grasp and catapulted over the dwarf. Twenty feet away he struck the first and second tufts of ground that the dwarf had just vacated. Fergus forgot to breathe.

Then McDougal was speeding past the grounded dragon. There was a flash of steel from McDougal's sword. A moment more and he was climbing the dead tree that tottered in the uncertain embrace of its neighbor. The dragon didn't follow, but seemed intent upon the dwarf before him.

Fergus let out his breath, and even allowed himself to smile. This was incredible, even surreal. He scrambled down the rock face and stepped up to the bog's edge. Lifting the bow, and swinging it to either side of the tree, he watched for the appearance of a Lyftfloga in flight, which might pluck his master from his perch.

As McDougal climbed twenty feet, then thirty feet, forty feet, and still no sign of a dragon, Fergus was unconsciously moving back and forth, when suddenly he tried to lift his foot and it would not follow his body. Looking down he saw the bog encircling both his feet, and thrusting himself backwards, he barely avoided disaster. There was a sucking smack of the mud as it reluctantly let go. The thought of being lost in that quagmire amongst blood leeches and suffocation sent his heart racing, and pity welled within him for the woeful soul—the dwarf, who was descending into its hideous death.

He had only looked away for a moment. Chastising himself for his neglected duty, Fergus raised his eyes to an empty tree.

No, it could not be. His heart beat thundered in his ears. Everything seemed to happen in slow motion, and strangely he found himself wondering how one's own heart could be so deafening.

He began sidestepping, eyes and bow trained on the spot where he had last seen his master. As he finally caught a glimpse of McDougal's leg amidst the branches, he relaxed slightly. Only, it was too late to save himself.

Twenty feet behind, a Lyftfloga bore down upon him. Worse yet, as he tried to turn and face the snorting fury, his feet would not pull free from the mire he had inadvertently tread upon.

Gimcrack

Distance was needed to fire a shot, but the beast was upon him so fast that there was only one way to regain enough space to allow for it. Instinctively Fergus twisted his body and fell backwards. Pulling and releasing the bowstring almost simultaneously as the lyftfloga soared along his body, raking it with outstretched claws. Some cut through his leather armor. There was searing pain and then a jerk. For an instant he was lifted inches above the swamp. Then the dragon burdened with the weight retracted its claws and let Fergus fall flat against the bog. He was now ten feet from its edge, upon his back, and hoping the arrow he had let fly would dissuade the Lyftfloga from further attack.

But there he lay, helpless. As of yet, his head rested upon the tenuous slime that crested the quagmire beneath. Any movement might begin his descent. Slowly he turned his head at a grunt from the forest. And there he saw McDougal, alive. He was pushing against the massive dead tree.

Slowly at first, the tree began to move. McDougal's body, holding the strain of its weight, seemed ready to snap. Now Fergus understood what McDougal was doing—he was sending the tree across the bog-land to make a sort of bridge.

A loud crack.

And then the dead tree broke free, and swung wild—it would fall far from the mark, useless. McDougal clung to the tree, as if he were breaking a wild horse. He somehow managed to draw his sword.

Fergus shut one eye as the muck oozed around it, and closed the corner of his mouth to keep it from seeping in. Still he watched the tree—something held it back for a moment, swaying unnaturally—a rope secured to a nearby oak. McDougal had tied it off. And so the tree deflected back around towards the bodies rooted in the bog. McDougal swung his blade. The rope severed, and the tree accelerated towards them.

It seemed as if the dwarf would be crushed, McDougal would fall to his death, and Fergus would watch it all, miserably, before joining them: his would be a slow suffocation.

But the dwarf was spared by inches as the massive tree boomed along his side. Perfectly still he stood, trapped in the mire up to his chest—black slime splattered across him—motionless except for the tears that left white trails upon his cheek. Beyond, crouched at the edge of the bog was the first Lyftfloga, a reminder that more than mud sought their demise. Curiously, it also moved not at all.

And McDougal—he had tried scrambling down the trunk as it fell—within seconds he was running along its length while it plunged, and then he had disappeared over the far edge, still high in the air.

After the sudden violence, all was quiet. Tree, mud, fallen men, and then the faintest sound of the gurgling stream. McDougal would spring up at any moment and pull them free. But minutes past, and nothing happened.

A slight shadow flitted across the dwarf.

Fergus felt the mire lick at his nose, and he was forced to turn his head towards the sky, to keep his nose and mouth clear. And there he saw the Lyftfloga circling against the sun. No doubt watching as its meal was slipping under.

Fergus could still see the dwarf from his periphery. Was that a branch within his reach? And so he called to him, "Climb out, man."

But the dwarf did not move.

"Climb out. There's a branch near enough to grab."

Still, he did not move. Speaking as he did started the suction in earnest, and so he tipped his head back to free his mouth for one last try. Fergus's eyes and even his nose dropped beneath the mud. But as soon as he opened his mouth, the bog silenced him. He held his breath, and fought with everything he could muster, inadvertently forcing himself deeper into the slime. And then Fergus called out to God, startled that he had not done so sooner—ashamed that he had not done so sooner.

His lungs felt as if they would burst, he gulped, swallowing nonexistent air. He knew it would not help, but he couldn't stop himself, so he gulped again.

Then something thrust itself into his side. Reaching along his body, he felt and grabbed it. As soon as he did, it pulled away, and he with it.

Fergus could breathe—oh blessed air of the Creator. Half blinded by the muck, he could make out a black figure, braced upon the fallen tree, dragging him through the mire. It was the dwarf.

"You're a good man and I thank you," Fergus said.

The dwarf's white teeth showed bright against his muddied face. It was half a smile, and his eye twitched. But Fergus would not judge a man for being afraid as long as he did his duty.

Fergus pulled himself up onto the tree, balancing easily on its wide trunk. "Back to back, now follow me."

As they approached the far side of the bog, Fergus watched the still motionless dragon. It stared at the spot where the dwarf had first fallen, and then he saw why—its head was no longer attached to its body.

The dwarf laughed nervously. Trembling, he shook his mace at the creature. Fergus heard him whisper, "You confounded beastie thing."

And then they saw McDougal, lying upon the ground, eyes blinking rapidly towards the sky. His sword lay at his side, white knuckles grasping the hilt. It reminded Fergus of someone trying to wake from a deep sleep, bewildered between dream and wakefulness.

The ground was solid beneath him. There was no blood. There was no enemy. There was no branch crushing the life from him. He simply lay there.

"I was waiting," McDougal said. "What took you so long?"

"I fell in the bog."

"That's nice."

"Yes, sir, it wasn't too bad."

"What about our friend?"

"He's here, sir, standing next to me. He got me out."

"Oh, that's very good; he's a worthy chap then."

"Yes, sir, and it was you who saved him, saved us both, sir."

"That's nice." McDougal's eyes closed. Fergus reached towards him when McDougal suddenly called out, "Where are the ladies? Are they safe? Keep them safe until I'm myself again."

"There are no ladies here, sir."

"Not here?"

"No, sir, we've been traveling alone."

"Oh. Well then I'll just take a little nap."

"Yes, sir, you do that, sir—I'll make ready our camp."

The dwarf pulled upon Fergus's sleeve as McDougal's eyes rolled shut. "If he sleeps now, he might not wake up, ever."

"What are you talking about?" Fergus asked. "He looks fine."

"Looks can be deceiving," the dwarf said. He leaned forward, lowering his voice, "He hasn't moved at all. His back could be broken, or a hundred bones shattered making him a shell of goo, or he could be bleeding, but inside the skin, so we can't see it. And he's sleepy in the middle of the day."

"What's that matter?"

"If a knock to the head makes a person tired when they shouldn't be, and you let them sleep, they might not wake up for days, if at all. I've seen it before. I don't like the look of it. I can barely see him breathing."

Fergus fumbled at his wine-skin and poured half its contents over McDougal's face. McDougal sputtered and shook his eyes open. "Are you trying to drown me, Fergus?"

"No, sir, I thought I would wake you."

"Is this how you'll be waking me from now on?"

"No, sir, it's just that you were sleeping."

"That's what I set out to do. Can't I sleep if I want to?"

"Of course, sir, I mean no, sir, I mean your brain is addled and you're out of your mind at the moment."

"Oh ..." McDougal cocked his head to one side, and then began moving his eyebrows up and down.

The dwarf stepped closer. "Lord McDougal, my name is Gimcrack, and I'm much honored to be at your service. I'll not forget what you've done for me."

"Very nice, indeed," McDougal said. "What are your skills, your occupation? Perhaps I can be of assistance if you're in need of any." Still McDougal didn't move.

"Yes, my Lord, I'm a map maker and engineer." Gimcrack stretched to his full dwarven height as he looked from McDougal to Fergus. "But my great love is to invent. First and foremost I'm an inventor."

"Did you hear that, Fergus?" McDougal asked. "We're in great need of inventors, aren't we? ... Yes, I'm sure of it. Hire him on as our inventor. That's if you're not already engaged."

"No, sir." Gimcrack eyed the dark woods. "I'll join your party, and wages won't be necessary."

"Good. Now, Fergus, as far as the ladies are concerned, please tell them I'll be myself once again tomorrow. Do whatever you can to make them comfortable. Give them rooms overlooking the river."

"But, sir, there are no ladies here."

"No ladies? I thought I heard a woman screaming, and didn't you say we saved her."

"No, sir, that was Gimcrack here who you saved. You just engaged him as your inventor."

"Oh, yes, excellent, excellent." McDougal studied Gimcrack's frame.

Now both of the Dwarf's eyes were twitching. He began rubbing at them furiously.

"But, he's a stout fellow, who was screaming like a girl?"

Gimcrack's fingers stopped, and slid down his face pulling his lower lip with them. His face was red—from rubbing or embarrassment it was hard to tell.

"There was no girl, sir," Fergus said. "I believe the screams you heard may have come from Gimcrack, sir." McDougal stared at him, not convinced.

"Okay, it was me. Please stop torturing me." Gimcrack fell to one knee. "But I'm no coward. It was the boy. He did it to me. A week ago I was a little nervous perhaps, occasionally high-strung even, but no coward. And then I met that boy, that boy."

Cozen Sacrifice

The next day McDougal was sitting up chewing his breakfast. He had slept a long time, and Fergus had watched and waited—hovering in prayer over his master.

"Taste and see that the Lord is good," McDougal said. "Though the Lord give you the bread of adversity, and the water of affliction, His ways are not man's ways, and as for me, I will praise His name." There was that great big grin again, and tears as well—but for once Fergus didn't mind them.

Gimcrack stopped what he was doing and sat down.

"Fergus, where is the little boy," McDougal said. "I can't remember what he looks like."

"A boy, sir?"

"Yes, the one who came with Gimcrack."

"He mentioned a boy, but there was no boy with him."

"Oh, I thought we met a nervous, scared little boy."

Gimcrack stood up and walked away from the fire.

"No, sir," Fergus said quietly. "Gimcrack's the nervous one."

The wind rustled through the woods. Gimcrack stopped, one foot hovering above the ground. He took a step backwards, spun on his heels, and walked quickly back to the camp.

Fergus suppressed a frown. McDougal suppressed a grin.

"The boy's name is Thiery," Gimcrack said. "He's only twelve or thirteen, so I don't place much blame on him, but they must have used him to trick me. I'd seen the boy on occasion around the animal pens, feeding them and the like. I'd never spoken to him, and he never to me. One day I was passing the horses, and the boy caught my attention.

"'Gimcrack, sir,' he says, 'that's the horse right there.'

"I looked at the beautiful creature, and thought to myself what it would be like to own something so wonderful. But then I realized I'd never talked to this boy in my life—about horses or anything else. 'What are you —'

"'I know you had your eye on her, sir, but she's not healthy.'

"I thought he must have mistook me for someone else. But he called me by name, and there weren't many dwarves on the expedition. Then I saw that his eyes were wide and full of other meanings.

"'What's wrong with her?' I asked.

"'She's sweet as can be, but very dangerous for someone to ride,' he said. 'I wouldn't take her even if she was a gift.'

"I thought maybe the boy had something wrong with him. He was earnest, but not making a bit of sense.

Then one of them Dragon Priests came out from the woods nearby. It startled me, and the boy too.

"'I can't right now, Gimcrack, sir,' the boy said. 'Come back tomorrow and I'd be happy to.' And then he slipped under the fence and led the animal away.

"It seemed that the priest smiled at me from under his hood. I'd much rather they continued to ignore me, but I smiled back as best I could.

"The next day the boy was there again.

"'You don't know God do you?' He asked. 'The God of Noah, the Most High.'

"'If you mean do I worship him?' I replied, 'then no, but I've heard of him.'

"Then that crazy boy clutched my hand, begging me with his eyes. 'You must follow him and no other god. They're all lies.' He pointed at the charm that hung about my neck. 'That goes to Hell, and you too, unless you give your soul to God.'

"'Don't talk like that boy.' I began the shivers. 'Now look what you've done to me. Have you cursed me?'

"'No, sir,' he whispered. 'You've been chosen, and I don't want you to die in your sins.'

"'You crazy boy, stop it, stop it!' I cried.

"He let go then and with a sharp stick began writing in the dirt. I wanted to get far away, but I stayed rooted to the spot. As soon as he finished, he stood up and erased the letters with his boot. But not before I saw it. And I believed him. Then he spoke the words that terrorize me to this very moment.

"'Be not afraid of them that kill the body, and after that have no more that they can do.' Then he clasped his arms about me and spoke into my ear. 'But I will forewarn you whom you shall fear: fear Him, which after He has killed has power to cast into Hell.'

"What kind of boy talks like that? Ever since then I have felt the flames of Hell compassing me about. Death's shadow is as my own, and the fear of it makes all my bones to shake.

"I ran from the spot and threw myself down within my tent. All I could think of was escape. But how? If an unknown but possible death awaited me within the company of a small army, it was a most probable death that awaited me, alone in the wilderness. I fell asleep, and dreamt of the priests.

"I awoke suddenly to my tent flap opening.

"It was still dark outside, but morning's light was just beginning. I steadied myself for the blow, but it didn't come. Instead there was a rasping voice, a whisper filled with wet gravel. 'The boy sent a gift for you, take it and flee.'

"Then the flap closed, and something breathed heavily. I gathered my things in a moment, and peered out. There in the dark stood the horse. I let her smell me, and rubbed along her neck and back. She was saddled. I looked about, not certain what to do. Hadn't the boy said not to take her? Was it the boy's to give? I hardly thought that possible. Then I heard the chanting of priests from somewhere to my right. That was all I needed.

"In a moment I was riding from the camp. The chanting was louder, and I looked back to see their wraith like forms in the moonlight. One of them laughed, and then the drum.

"It thrummed like a heartbeat, slow at first, then faster and faster, and then nothing. I let the horse have its way, trusting her in the darkness. It didn't take long to realize we were being hunted. As the dragons pressed in, I don't know if I was more afraid or that horse, that poor beautiful horse."

"What was it," McDougal asked, "that the boy wrote in the dirt?"

Gimcrack looked over his shoulder, towards the bog and then into the woods, rubbing the charm about his neck. "Cozen Sacrifice. He wrote the words Cozen Sacrifice." Gimcrack wheezed an uneasy laugh. "But, they didn't get me. And as long as they don't find out I might be okay."

"Thanks be to God," McDougal said, "and no doubt to the prayers of that courageous boy. But tell me, what is this Cozen Sacrifice?"

"Dragon cultists who sacrifice in this way gain witching powers and rewards from Marduk, the sun god. The sun lightens the world, and the serpent, the dragon, is the one who enlightened our forefathers to know good and evil and to know that they could be like gods. One of Marduk's sacred animals is the dragon, the deceiver, who enlightens the world as does the sun. But the sun does not just give light and life. It can also burn and bring death. This, the dragon loves to do, and if through deception all the better. So the greater the deception the more witching power Marduk gives. But the sacrifice must end in death."

"We've not seen these dragon cultists before," McDougal said. "But we have heard of Marduk. Isn't that his symbol on your charm?"

"It is. But I don't follow the dragon's path; I follow the bull's path as do many who worship Marduk. He has a dark side and a light side. I follow the light, and fear the dark."

"It sounds like a dangerous business," McDougal said, dubiously. "I must tell you that both the light and the dark of this god of yours are lies, and the path you've chosen does lead to Hell, exactly as the boy has told you. The Most High God commands that no images be made of Him so that we don't corrupt ourselves by worshiping His creation. No images of men or women, of beasts in the earth or winged creatures in the air, of things that creep upon the ground or fish in the waters. And that we don't lift our eyes unto heaven to worship the sun or the moon, and serve them as you have done. An abomination to God it is, and He has forbidden it. Listen well, my friend; you can have that bone-trembling fear taken away."

"How?" For now Gimcrack was shaking again.

"By doing what the boy said. Repent of these false gods, and give your heart and soul to the one true God. Then it is heaven and eternal life that awaits you at your death, whenever that might be."

27

"I don't know. I need to think," Gimcrack said, still trembling.

"There's something I'd like to know," Fergus said. "Why do you think the boy tricked you?"

"He gave me the horse, didn't he?"

"He warned you not to take it. He must have known that the Lyftfloga were about the encampment and somehow knew of their plan to sacrifice you. Whoever gave you the horse said it was from the boy, but you said yourself, he could hardly have been in a position to give it away, and not only that, but if he was trying to help you, and I believe he was, then the Dragon Priests must know it."

All three were silent. Gimcrack cradled his head in his arms. McDougal unsheathed his sword and honed its edge. And Fergus waited for his lord to speak.

In a few minutes he did.

"Whatever the boy's intentions," McDougal said, "he claims the Most High, and it's our duty to help him. I'll be well enough to travel in a day or two. Fergus, please let the ladies know of our plans."

Adoption

It was dark. The night creatures were all but finished with their hunting, making way for the beasts of the day. The sentries prepared to be relieved, and one tent, larger than the rest, glowed and danced from the firelight within. If he went, it had to be now. The camp was hushed, and at this time of day, almost peaceful.

Thiery liked to make a game of it. Mouse-like he would scurry from the stables to tents, hiding from an owlish sentry. Wolf-like he would study their movements, keeping to the shadows, ready to make a bold face if cornered.

What would he say if they caught him? They never had, but what would he say? The best thing would probably be to call out, "Oded the Bear, I'm with Oded the Bear." Thiery smiled as he imagined the sentry poised to strike him down, then faltering upon hearing that great name. Oded—the greatest ranger there ever likely was.

Thiery was close enough now to hear Suzie singing from within the meal tent. It was a soft sound, filled with simple words telling God how much she loved Him. She would often thank Him in her songs for the food she was preparing, and for Flemup and Elvodug the cooks.

In their presence, she was like a pearl before swine. There were filth smudges upon all they touched, and the odor—what a smell it was! Flemup and Elvodug's specialty was in the night-soil, cleaning human waste from the cesspools back at Bannockburn Castle and its township and selling it as fertilizer.

They also ran the death cart. They rejoiced when times of famine or war were afoot, for then business was good. And Flemup could be hired as a corpse-bobber, cramming several bodies into a grave by jumping up and down upon them.

This, Elvodug refused to do, though both were bone-pickers and grave robbers, unearthing trinkets from the dead.

These were the men who touched and prepared the army's food. Needless to say, they were quite unpopular, with the stench and grime festering upon their persons. Even more so since their bland meals became infected, through association, in the minds of those who ate them. That was, until Elvodug enlisted the child to help with the cooking. He said she was a distant, unwanted relation. And so Elvodug masqueraded as 'Uncle Elvodug', his preferred title, but Suzie and Thiery knew the truth.

The child, as Elvodug and Flemup called her, was known to the rest as Suzie. And though priest fear engulfed the camp when Oded the bear or Thiery mentioned the God of Noah, Suzie sang and spoke as if she never noticed the Dragon Priests and their cultists scowling, or the troubled glances from those who followed Marduk, and Mithras, and others.

Suzie seemed to hold the Most High's hand wherever she went, and it caused the warrior priests and the rest of the army to pause. In any event, their stomachs told them that she could stay.

For a moment, Suzie's voice grew loud enough for Thiery to hear more than just the melody. His heart warmed at the blending of her voice with words of praise:

I will say of the Lord,
He is my refuge and my fortress:
my God; in Him will I trust.

He shall cover thee with His feathers,
and under His wings shalt thou trust:
His truth shall be thy shield and buckler.

Thou shalt not be afraid
for the terror by night;
nor for the arrow that flieth by day:

For He shall give His angels
charge over thee,
to keep thee in all thy ways

Thou shalt tread upon the lion and adder:
the young lion and the dragon

shalt thou trample under feet.

She was a bold one singing like that with Dragon cultists on every side. He wondered if any lay in the dark of their tents, foreheads creased—grinding their teeth.

Thiery glided through the last open space and ducked inside. He puckered his nose and moved away from the sleeping forms of Elvodug and Flemup. Suzie turned from the stewing pots and beamed.

"Oh, Thiery, I knew you'd be here soon. I've been talking to God about you."

"Thank you, Suzie, and a God-blessed morning to you."

"I've got some food scraps from yesterday for the puppy." Suzie tossed them into Thiery's bag as he opened it.

"This will do nicely, and I have some news. Yesterday he let me scratch his head as he ate. It's going very well; Oded says I might have him as my own within the week, and he seems to grow every day a little bigger. I would like for you to come with me and see him; he's taller than me. Oded thinks he'll be big enough for a man to ride, a full grown man. But already he could carry you."

Suzie's tiny body twittered as she hop-skipped about the pots, clapping her hands, and giggling. "Oh, how exciting! I like the name Horatio. Will you name him that?"

"That seems a noble name." Thiery thought a bit, and then smiled. "I will, Suzie, for you. The food you've given him, I think that's what's done it so quick, so it's only right that his name should come from you also."

"Wonderful, just oh so wonderful. I don't dare wake Uncle Elvodug to ask him, but maybe I could go tomorrow for a very, very little while. But what of all the beasties in the woods? Why don't they eat you, Thiery?"

Thiery laughed. "Well for certain, because God has not allowed for me to be eaten. And Oded has shown me that the squirrel and the mouse, the birds and the badger all have their enemies to be sure. But still they amble about the woods. They're aware and quick-witted, ready to run at the first sign of danger. And like the badger, I'm not without a mean bite if I'm cornered, for Oded has taught me well—though I'm young—to use my spear, and my bow. He says that it is the young ones, if they can but learn God's wisdom for the woods, which make the best Rangers when they're older. And I don't wander too far from the Big Bear's reach. So you see I have every hope not to be eaten."

"I don't believe," Suzie said, "that God will allow me to be eaten tomorrow either. If only he'll soften Elvodug's heart to let me go."

"Let me have something of yours that holds your scent, so Horatio will know you better when you meet."

"Oh, you are very smart, Thiery." Suzie loosened her cloth belt and handed it over. "This is so exciting! Please tell Horatio that I am very happy to meet him. Will you tell him that?"

"I will."

Just then Flemup made some revolting noises: he belched, he snorted, he mumbled. Elvodug responded by thrashing about and then speaking in his sleep. "Drowning, drowning, throw me a line, quick you fool, drowning."

Flemup called back, "Look at that meat. We can't serve that."

Elvodug seemed to forget that he was drowning, and decided to inquire about the meat. "Why not?" He sat up in bed, but still his eyes were closed.

"Why not? You idiot. Maggots is why not. There's more maggots than there is meat."

"You say maggots, I say grain," Elvodug said. "We'll make a beef and barley soup." They both chuckled in their sleep.

"You're a genius," Flemup said, smiling. And then they both settled into a patterned snore.

Thiery and Suzie stood motionless, giggling between their fingers. After a while, Thiery whispered into the silence, "I said I had news, and I saved the best for last. I've been thinking about how you and I are both foundlings. Do you know what a foundling is?"

"Someone who's been found?"

"Well, hopefully that's what happens to a foundling. But, they're children without parents, orphans."

"Oh, so I guess we are then."

"Yep, but new parents can adopt you into their family, and then you're no longer a foundling."

"But haven't you been adopted into Oded's family?"

"No, he's my guardian. My mother, before she died, appointed him. There's something secret about it that I'm not allowed to know until I'm sixteen, or until one of my guardians feel that it's absolutely necessary that I'm told sooner."

"One of your guardians? Who else guardians you?"

"I don't know. It's a secret."

"Oh, that sounds exciting."

"I suppose it is, but what I wanted to say is that every foundling hopes for a family, right?"

"Oh, yes."

"Do you think of Elvodug and Flemup as having adopted you into their family?"

"No." Tears threatened her tiny face.

"We both know that they aren't the kindest of men. Suzie, it's not right for you to be so alone in the world. When the time is right, I'd like to find you a better place."

"But I'm not alone. I have God. He's a Father to them without one, and I have you."

"That's exactly right, and so, Suzie, if you'd have me, I'd like to adopt you as my sister. Then together maybe we could find some parents to make us a true family. I've told Oded all about it and he thinks it's a grand idea—he'd like to bop those two thieves on the head. And don't you worry, even if you say no, I'll always do my best to keep you safe and take care of you. But God knows, I'd be mightily pleased to have a sister like you."

Suzie straightened up on her toes, clapping her tiny hands. Thiery took that for a yes.

Elvodug called out again in his sleep, and then sat up while rubbing his eyes. Thiery darted from the tent with a wave of his hand to Suzie.

He neared the cave. In the distance he thought he heard the quickening beats of a drum. And maybe a horse neigh. But then they both stopped, and maybe they had never been.

A fitful wind disturbed the quiet, covering the soft noises he might make, but it also masked the threat looming in the dark. Through the forest canopy, he could no longer see the stars, but instead of morning-glow, a cloud-horde raced across the sky. It was a power-ful sight. Would God unleash a storm, or was it passing by on some other errand? Thiery smiled up at God's wonder, and thought of Suzie's song.

"Can I see your wing?" He whispered to his God. "Or the Angel who watches me, Lord?"

Just then his eyes caught a movement from the cave mouth to his right.

At the same time he sensed, maybe saw, something to his left.

Terror by night?

His heart hammered, "run!" But he stood very still.

He could just see the cave, maybe a hundred feet away. In the black of its entrance, lips curled back exposing snarled teeth. There was a low growl that Thiery could see but not hear because of the wind-whipped trees. The teeth came a little closer and now there was a smattering of white fur, and he knew it was the wolf pup.

Then he strained his eyes far to the left without turning his head; a lightning strike shattered. Thiery's ears rang, and the very earth seemed to reel from the blow. The racing clouds lit like a swirling sea and it appeared that the world was upside down. The cave, forest, and river all showed bright for an instant only. And in the moment of complete darkness that followed, Thiery was momentarily blinded.

Yet he could see an imprint in his mind of that dazzling display. In the fading light lines that resembled trees he saw the night terror, lurking, ready to strike.

If he could not see, then the creature might still be blinded too. Leaving his back exposed, he turned to where he had last remembered the cave, and the wolf, and refuge. He swung his spear about, laying it across his shoulder with its point protruding behind him—that would be his bite, though a small one. He still could not see well, but he sped towards the cave with the blunt spear end affording some protection against the rocks ahead.

Behind him, it was coming, and worse it was gaining.

But the cave, he knew, was close. Thiery lunged forward as he half imagined half felt the breath of the beast upon his neck. His spear hit something hard, and his sweating fingers slipped along its length. His face struck rock.

Stunned, he tottered and fell.

The savage, growling form of the wolf leaped passed him, as if from the rock itself.

Thiery reached out to pull himself up, but there was nothing there—off balance he tumbled forward and into the cave. The wolf's growling continued but for a moment, and something else too, something terrible.

Then the wolf sprung in beside him, and they both edged deeper. Thiery gripped his knife in one hand and touched the bristling back of the wolf with the other. The night terror's bulk could not follow.

Once again lightning crackled and lit the outside, a great leathery form, maybe a leg or arm, or body, showed glistening in the rain, and then the dark came back. The next time the lightning broke there was nothing but trees.

Soon the winds died down, and the wolf relaxed.

"We're okay now, boy, we're okay." He didn't know if he said it more for the wolf or for himself. Grinning, he realized the wolf had saved him; the wolf had joined in what Oded called pack brotherhood. What's more, it had held the night terror at bay—just long enough to let Thiery escape—cunning for such a young one. Thiery would now call it by name. The name Suzie had asked for. It had a noble sounding out—Horatio, the wolf cub, worthy of kings.

It was an hour before Thiery crept from his burrow. His spear lay upon the ground where it had fallen.

"I'll not let go so easy next time," Thiery said. "But it was a scary thing." Wolf and boy peered out from the cave mouth, not quite ready to leave. No more wind or clouds. The sun scattered through the trees with a reddish gleam.

"Thanks, Horatio, you're a brave boy." Thiery patted his head. "God willing, I'll see you again tomorrow." And then he ran.

Darting among the trees, in and out, this way and that, ever mindful that something was out there. In minutes he was back to the encampment, to the animal pens, looking for Oded. They hadn't been cared for. Would Oded be angry at the delay? Surely not after he explained. But Oded wasn't with the horses, or the hounds, and so he set to work, all the time watching and waiting.

Father

"**B**oy." A bony finger beckoned from the folds of the priestly robe.

Thiery hadn't heard the priest come up. He was afraid of them, yet curious too.

Once, Oded had sent Thiery scurrying up a tree, when the sounds of battle marched upon the wind. Oded had then run with his war hounds to break their right flank. Thiery climbed higher and higher until he saw that the priests were fighting like mad men alongside the other warriors. Their hoods were thrown back, maces pounding against the enemy, but what had caused Thiery to white-knuckle grip the branch he held was something all together different than he had ever seen or heard.

The priests banshee-screamed, sending a chill through him, as if they were some creatures from another world. Occasionally their voices came together in freakish song, at which point it sounded like demons joining their hellish chorus. Wherever they struck, the foe's ranks would bend and twist to get away.

But what struck him most was that their skin was blue, at least mostly blue.

So that, now, Thiery found himself searching into the deep hood of the priest, terrified at what he might see. It may have been blue, but all he could really tell was that it was dark, the whites about the eyes seemed to glow like a creature of the night.

Thiery remembered his God and gained courage. "Sir, may I feed the hounds first? Oded might not be pleased if I were to leave them without their breakfast."

"It's Oded I've come to speak to you about. Follow me, and touch no one."

And so he walked behind the priest's flowing robes, wondering what it all meant. The rows of tents around Oded's and Thiery's were gone, except for one other tent adjacent to theirs. More priests stood near.

Further out, many warriors watched, weapons raised in salute. Was it him they were giving honors to, but why? There was something else strange. As he looked upon their faces, he saw fear.

Count Rosencross—master of faraway Bannockburn Castle, leader of two hundred men—sat perfectly still upon his mount. They say he was born upon the saddle. His black armor seemed to meld with the black of his war charger.

Thiery looked up at the priest's white eyes, wondering but afraid to speak.

"Oded has the wasting sickness." The priest pointed at their tent. "You can choose. We can burn you now, and you die, bold and in your strength. Or you can set about the waiting, and see if it gets you too. You've been much in his company, sharing his tent and food."

He wanted to ask if Oded might still live, but he knew tears would come with the asking. "But I don't feel sick."

"You have been with Oded."

"God will keep me," Thiery said. "Whatever happens, whether he heals Oded and me or not, I'm His. I'll not choose the burning." And then he turned and walked into his tent.

Later that day there was the sound of feet approaching, something set down, and a hurrying away. Thiery hoped it was food, for his belly was beginning to ache.

Even before he opened the tent-flap, wonderful smells began wafting through. Suzie must have prepared it special. Not only was there a steaming meat pie, but a cooked apple with sugar and butter. This waiting might not be so bad.

What should he expect with the wasting sickness anyway? It must come on awful fast, for Oded looked his usual strength just last night. And so Thiery ate as quick as may be, fearing his appetite might leave when the sickness began.

Then disaster struck. Not having any experience with a cooked apple, Thiery carried it to his mouth—eyes closed to savor the first bite—when the weight of it suddenly disappeared.

Opening his eyes in astonishment, all he held was the soft peel, with a great hole in its bottom. Exploded upon the ground were bits and pieces of its center, turning the dirt to apple mud.

Thiery often practiced giving thanks through adversity, but this was one of his most difficult tests yet. Just yesterday he had seen the head table being served the same wonderful dessert, and now his was ruined.

Setting the peel carefully upon his plate, he dropped to his knees, licking and nibbling the least affected morsels: delicious despite the occasional crunch of soil. Then he grabbed up the apple skin in both hands, and sitting upon his sleeping furs, he decided to give some ceremony to the remaining treat.

Thiery held the peel captive before his eyes. "Some of you have escaped, but don't think for a minute that I'll be so careless again. What's that? You beg for mercy ..."

Then a curious thing occurred. For the slightest instant, it seemed as if the apple moved. Thiery stared hard, thinking that maybe he should drop it. But oh, how he wanted to eat. There it was again, the apple did move.

Thiery shook his head, and the ground swayed under him. Steadying one arm on the furs he continued the game. "What trick is this you play?" Only, those words didn't come. Instead a jumbled groan spilled forth. His tongue felt too big.

He was afraid. Thiery tried to let himself down easy, but the ground came at him fast, and he saw no more.

Thiery could not tell how long he had lain unconscious. He stirred his mind and body to work. His body refused, but his mind began to respond.

Was it real or dream, or maybe part way in between? He knew that place, when one began to climb from sleep, and then unwittingly slipped back into dreams—yet thinking all the while he bided with the waking. Sometimes, in those early morning hours he would run all the way to the white wolf, or to the food tent visiting Suzie, or to 'make water', only to find he had been dreaming—yet it would seem so very real.

That was where Thiery sensed he might be now. There was a horse riding hard, closer and closer it came, until he could hear it breathing heavy outside the tent. A voice spoke out which he recognized as the deep hale of Count Rosencross.

"What do you here, priest?" Rosencross demanded.

"I say goodbye to my son," The priest said. His voice seemed familiar, high pitched and nasal. Maybe it was the one who met him while feeding the hounds.

"Does he yet live, then?"

"No, my Lord, by now he must be gone, I just wanted a moment."

There was a long silence. Thiery tensed to move, to speak, but nothing. Could this be death? No, he did not think so. God loves the death of His saints, and surely He would be there to meet Thiery or have sent some Angels for that purpose. Thiery's fear left him as he waited upon the Lord.

"It's a hard thing, priest," Rosencross said.

"It is that, and he died not ever knowing who I was, but the deception draws near, and what better ..." The priest stopped suddenly. "Think of the Dragon, besides Oded poisoned the boy's mind in the way."

"Enough for me," Rosencross said as he mounted. "Don't stay over long. Oded returns soon and we must make ready."

It was quiet again. His mind whirled in confusion, and then the tears came. A boy's dream of a valiant father—whom he would one day find—went shipwreck upon his young heart.

The Cave

When Thiery next woke he told his eyes to open. They did, but slowly. The sun shone upon the tent. It was uncomfortably warm.

He sat up, stiff, and his head pounded with the effort.

He tried to swallow. Wincing from the pain, he felt the desire to swallow again, but this time he must have water first. His water skin lay at his feet—empty. And then he realized that he could hear the river. Usually, he could only hear it while the encampment slept, for the two hundred soldiers, and priests, and baggage train drowned out most everything.

How long had he slept? Now he noticed the hunger. The sugared apple and its peel lay on the ground, covered with ants.

Dead ants.

Then his thoughts and memories fevered upon him: Adopting Suzie, the night terror and Horatio fighting it off, the priest and the whole encampment looking at him.

He had passed out.

Oded sick. But was he? Count Rosencross said something about him returning. The unknown priest ... his father?

He tried to swallow, forgetting that it would hurt, and this time it felt like a pricker bush stuck in his throat. Slinging his water skin over his shoulder, he grabbed his spear and slowly pulled the tent flap aside. Nothing. He poked his head out.

All around was trampled dirt, with a few tufts of grass here and there. No tents, no horses or hounds, no army. Thiery stood alone in the clearing—the woods and the river and the hills ringed about. And all the creatures they contained.

Thiery stepped back inside and gathered what few belongings there were: his bow, six arrows, sleeping furs, flint pack, and a heavy cloak. Running to the river he drank deeply, filled his water skin, then drank again. Up stream, some deer were doing the same. This would be a good place to hunt, or be hunted. For now though, his limbs felt strange, and very weak; he needed a safe place to rest.

"Horatio, Horatio?" Thiery called out and then whistled, though not too loud. But the wolf didn't come. Thiery stood at the entrance and felt a slight air current pulling in. That was good. Fresh air would constantly enter and it had to go somewhere.

He gathered branches and dead leaves, and worked his way back into the cave. The passage was small at first so that he had to stoop slightly, but as he went further it widened, and the ground began to rise.

Waiting for his eyes to grow accustomed to the dark, he reached down and felt the earth. It was dust dry, and that was best of all. A dry cave would make a good home, even if it was only temporary—for in a few days he planned on tracking the army, and finding his sister and Oded, and try to make sense of what had happened. Maybe he could somehow meet his father. He would gain strength and train with Horatio first.

Soon, firelight was playing upon the rock, and Thiery was astonished to see a large domed chamber ahead. To his great satisfaction he watched the smoke travel quickly towards the ceiling, and then suck suddenly out of sight over what might be a rock shelf along the cavern wall twenty feet above.

Thiery set about making a larger fire in the domed room. As that fresh flame lit the chamber, he saw that there were some natural hand holds for climbing to the ledge above, and some grips that looked man made—cut into the face of the rock. He was eager to climb.

But his weariness was overwhelming, and so laying out his bedding, he slept.

Sometime in the night he woke to find that the fire was out, and the darkness was like a place where panic and fear were birthed. Thiery called out to the Lord, speaking one of the songs Suzie often offered in praise, and he heard his voice strangely echoed.

"You make darkness, and it is night: wherein all the beasts of the forest do creep forth. You will light my candle: the Lord my God will enlighten my darkness. Yea, though I walk through the valley of the shadow of death, I will fear no evil: for thou art with me; thy rod and thy staff they comfort me." These words warmed his soul. He smiled up at his God, and suddenly noticed the faintest glow from the rock shelf above. Oh precious light! God's goodness shone up there. For the completeness of the dark was too much for him, young and alone.

Thiery reached for his water skin and took a drink. Replacing it, his hand brushed against his bed furs far from where he remembered that they should be. Stranger still, they were warm.

Then they moved.

Thiery drew his hand away and listened. The slightest hint of breathing. The smell of dog ... and then he knew. It was not a dog he smelled, but wolf. And so Thiery laid back, placed his arm about Horatio's neck, and did not wake till late in the morning.

Some daylight made its way through the cave mouth, and more light from beyond the ledge fairly illuminated the ceiling. Sitting up, he scratched Horatio behind the ears. Then he set to work making a fire.

"I'm so hungry I could eat Elvodug and Flemup's cooking," Thiery said to himself, smiling as he imagined how Oded would have laughed at the joke.

Most of the afternoon was spent spearing fish, cooking fish, and eating fish. Thiery was an eager student of

Oded the Bear. Being a ranger and beast-master besides, Oded was an important and valuable man. He thanked God every day, for putting it on the Bear's soft heart to take him in at only seven, and for his mother's choosing such a good and godly guardian. And now he would try to remember everything he had learned, and apply it with wisdom—one eye on the tasks at hand and one eye on the Most High. He would try and make Oded proud.

Food and shelter were taken care of. Now he could explore.

Looking to where the smoke disappeared above him, he grabbed a handhold in the rock and began the climb. Horatio whined and stood up on his hind legs.

"Don't worry, boy, I'm not leaving. Aren't you even curious what's up there?"

Thiery knew there might be danger just over the edge of that rock. Maybe snakes, or spiders, or it could be the lair of something else entirely. But what he found, he was unprepared for—a sword's point inches from his face, and in the shadows, the man who held it.

Ladies of Hradcanny

McDougal stood up suddenly. "Do you smell that?"

Gimcrack grabbed his mace.

McDougal slowly turned with his face straining upwards, sniffing, and filling his lungs. "Now, that is just an amazing smell, and notice how our clothes are warmed when He quiets the earth by the south wind, just amazing."

"My Lord," Gimcrack said, sniffing the air. "What exactly is it you smell?"

"Do you mean you don't know? It's on the wind. It's God's freshness cleaning the earth; drink it in while it lasts." McDougal breathed in deep again, closed his eyes and grinned.

Gimcrack looked at Fergus, raised his eyebrows, and angled his head towards McDougal.

"Excuse me, sir," Fergus said. "Your ways are yet unfamiliar to Gimcrack, and I fear he might think you unwell."

"Unwell?" McDougal jostled Gimcrack's shoulder and smiled. "I've never felt better. You know the smell, when you're indoors, and someone comes in, and they smell of the crisp outside. That's what I smell now, only it's stronger."

Gimcrack slowly sniffed the air. He looked everywhere but at McDougal. He sniffed again, and finally shrugged his shoulders.

McDougal chuckled. "Anyway, let's push on and find the boy, perhaps there'll be some adventure worthy of our swords."

McDougal began looking about the camp edges, but he was no tracker. His tall form was bent intently over the ground like a willow branch. He muttered "Hmm," and "interesting," and "that could be something."

"Perhaps, sir," Fergus said, "our map maker remembers the way."

"I had forgotten you were a map maker. By the Most High, we are blessed," McDougal said, beaming. "Well then, I'll give you the honor of guiding us."

"Yes, my Lord."

The rest of that day, whenever McDougal wasn't looking, Gimcrack strove to gain Fergus's attention with repeated throat clearings and not so subtle facial movements. At one point McDougal whispered to Fergus. "He's a more nervous sort of fellow than I thought, poor thing."

A little while later Gimcrack took his turn and leaned close to Fergus, saying something about muscle spasms and a bruised brain. Fergus pretended not to hear.

When McDougal began to walk in a more normal and relaxed fashion, Gimcrack's agitations increased, whispering to Fergus about the last burst of normalcy before the end comes. Fergus was also alarmed, but for a different reason.

McDougal was thinking, and thinking hard. But the discussion Fergus expected did not come.

"Fergus, the princes of the realm will all be in attendance," McDougal said. "Lords, ladies, lesser kings, they all gather within a fortnight."

"Yes, sir."

"And my pride wants to stay far from it. But my duty says I must tell the tale of what has happened, and that I should pay respects, even if I am the 'Dead Lord.'"

"That is as it should be, sir. But you're not dead yet."

"There is another reason. I am twenty nine now. I thought that come this year's feast I would ask for Strongbow's daughter."

Fergus struggled to keep his countenance in check. Rapid heartbeats, a swooning within his gut, and, he hoped, the rising warmth of his face did not show. "Forgive me, sir, but he is the High King, and your loyalties could not be doubted."

"What do you say, Fergus?"

"Just that there are other lords who are difficult, who Strongbow could bind to him with the Lady Catrina."

"You mean more powerful, more important." McDougal shrugged. "Regardless, last year, with the king's permission, I made my intentions known to her."

"But, you said nothing to me."

"I knew your feelings concerning the lady." McDougal looked sheepish. "I respect you, Fergus, and I didn't want to hear what you might say."

Fergus had thought that only God himself could have known, and now he realized that McDougal must perceive a good many things. There were clandestine looks and hushed words following his master's awkward form wherever he went—suddenly Fergus felt fiercely protective, and for the first time he could remember, he felt that his eyes might have that glassy look, surely not tears, but a heartache revealed there. He blinked.

"I'm sorry, sir. She is beautiful, but I was concerned. I'd not speak against her character, but there were certain things that I hoped for you. You see, she is often in the company of her cousin, and I could not help but see, differences ..."

McDougal smiled then. "Yes, none of us are perfect, but little Mercy is quite close."

"Yes, sir. And Lady Mercy is not so little any more, I dare say you may not toss her in the air this visit. She is nineteen now, and for years she has watched over and cared for everyone within the castle, regardless of position. She's greatly loved. And she serves the Most High."

"Now I see what bride you've chosen for me, but even Mercy is too high a mark for a landless lord. And that is why above all other reasons I must go to Hradcany. I must formally withdraw my courtship and put to rest any obligations the king or his daughter might feel concerning me."

"Begging your pardon, my Lord," Gimcrack interrupted, "but we are not far from the camp and I don't see or hear a thing."

54

They approached a lone tent with weapons drawn. Hung above the front was a black cloth. "Sickness," Gimcrack said. "They left someone behind."

McDougal swung the flap open with the flat of his sword. Inside it was empty, except for a shriveled apple skin, unusual in that it was surrounded by dead ants.

All there was to do was follow the trail-sign. The army was traveling towards the going down of the sun. The same way that led to Hradcanny. But the night was closing in upon the day, clouds had gathered, and distant thunder spoke of possible rain. So they took to the tent, and McDougal sang a song of the Most High. Gimcrack told of the sea, and the ships that he had sailed upon, and the great dwarven brotherhood to which he belonged, and soon, hoped to return.

"A story then. Let's have a story." McDougal directed his request to Gimcrack, who smiled and rubbed his hands together.

"Do you know the proper history of Tump Barrows?" Gimcrack asked.

McDougal and Fergus shook their heads. "We've heard some, but surely it's not the proper history, for no dwarf told us the tale."

Gimcrack's eyes sparkled. "For a century Strongbow's Father, Frothgar the mad, put us dwarven folk to work in the mines and caves that abound in this land, to dig, and toil, and bring him precious metals, but most of all we were to search for her." Gimcrack paused. He looked from McDougal to Fergus, making sure he had gained an attentive audience.

"Who were we searching for you ask? His queen, and Frothgar loved her much. But alas, as the way of all us mortals must go, she died, and still very young, and Frothgar went mad with despair. That was when Redwald, our very own dwarven bard, came to the court and sang to the king a song known as the epic of Tump Barrow. Frothgar discovered that your God of Noah banished those who would not serve Him to Sheol, the underworld of the dead.

"This greatly distressed the king, for he knew that his wife and he had turned their backs on Noah's God long ago. And he feared it was true. So, he locked up Redwald, and day after day, the king questioned him about the God of Noah, the underworld, and about his dead queen. Now Redwald is a bold fellow and he would not waiver, but told what he believed to be true, that Frothgar's queen, who worshipped the gods, was indeed one of the sufferers in Sheol."

"So, the king had Redwald killed then?" McDougal asked.

"Oh no, Redwald is still very much alive. King Frothgar, in his madness, sent slavers to capture and purchase dwarves from kingdoms near and far. He made Redwald a sort of overseer, and anyone who was less than five feet tall found themselves in the mines, creating a vast underground city for his queen. If we found her, we would be given a kingdom of our own above ground. But she was never found, for a hundred years Tump Barrows grew, for that is what we call the mines and caves. And now that Strongbow has freed us from our slavery, he has made us the keepers of our heritage, and Redwald the bard is now Lord Redwald of Tump Barrows."

"Fascinating! But the dwarves were freed almost ten years now. Why have I never heard of this Lord Redwald?" McDougal asked.

"Strongbow himself came into our little kingdom, and made Redwald a lord, and while other fiefdoms give grain and meat and some silver for the land and protection of their king, we provide him with much gold, silver, copper, rubies, iron ore and a mysterious realm with free passage to those he confides in. So the knowledge of Redwald and our Dwarven Brotherhood, while not entirely a secret, is not widely known either."

"I would very much like to meet this Lord Redwald of yours. Perhaps he could even be of service to us in finding the boy."

"When you have served one of the Dwarven Brotherhood you have served us all. And when someone shows us a kindness, we are careful to remember it. You say the word and I'll place my petition before him."

Rosencross

The Hilltop Inn loomed over the countryside, four stories of stone walls three feet thick and oaken doors reinforced with metal bands. Iron-grate windows were narrow near the ground, letting in little light, yet they grew wider with ornately etched glass the higher they rose.

Rooftop parapets leaned out over the hill, which declined to the highway, the road to Hradcany—a short day's travel. The rest of the hill's crest had been flattened, the dirt simply removed and piled around its perimeter forming an earthen berm, atop which a twenty foot palisade enclosed a courtyard—barns, stables, and a well.

Rosencross liked what he saw. Especially what could not be seen. Below the cellar was a dungeon, and below the dungeon were passages; it was a stage well set for the Dragon's work.

And he liked that the Dragon's reach was often invisible and full of force. His was the god of forces: for Rosencross and twenty of his party had merely arrived, given the sign and shown the marks, and the whole of the Hilltop Inn was placed at his disposal.

One evening, he paced within his chamber. Over and over he stopped at a silver framed mirror and admired his reflection. He was entombed in black, even his leather gauntlets and cape. Towering, he flexed muscles and watched approvingly as his armor swelled and creaked.

Yet there was a place upon the face of the mirror that he dared not look; he felt its beckoning call, its accusing stare. How could he enjoy the handsome presence before him with this going on? Enough then! Rosencross was no whimpering coward, and so he met with his own eyes, at once cold and penetrating, and then there was a twinge, a prick of the conscience—a feeling he especially disliked.

He must put a stop to it. He would find the Priest—his Priest—and then it would go away.

Down the winding stairs, boots scraping on wood worn smooth, past the tavern, down still until the oak changed to stone, and echoed taps came back hollow and distant. He had wound his way down, away from the meager lights, and into the dark.

"Are you here Priest?"

Rosencross heard the faintest movement. Cloth upon cloth—robes.

"I am here." The voice was much higher than his own, and nasal. Even when whispering as the Priest did now, it was conspicuous, and a part of him recoiled at the sound. "You have come because of the boy?"

Again the Priest anticipated his thoughts.

"Yes."

"You think he was an unworthy sacrifice then?" The Priest's voice was tight, disapproving.

"He was only a boy. Was there any challenge in bringing him down, any strength that we gained, any great deception foisted upon him that the Dragon will bless us for? And rangers are few enough, four years training, gone."

The Priest did not move, but Rosencross could hear his breathing, rapid and sharp. Then the striking sound of flint, and a candle burned between them, set on a niche protruding from the wall. The Priest held out his hands, palms down, and spoke, a little deeper, a little less nasal. "What do you see Count?"

"The marks."

"Yes, but tell me more."

"They cover you, there's not a place left."

The Priest liked that and his smile was genuine. "Yes, one serpent for each sacrifice. For each one that you've played a part, or that I've shared because of our singular association, I've stained blue."

Rosencross tried to stay calm, but he could not, his eyes flashed down—they were all blue. "You honor me Priest, I'm pleased"

"Good, then so am I. Now as to the boy, you said that he was valuable, or at least he would have been as a ranger and probably a beast-master. He was innocent of our deception, and this the Dragon desires. He was under the care of Oded the bear, yet we stole him away. And he was my son ... my loyalty then is etched in blood and stone. He was the last of my children. All have been sacrificed to the Dragon. But most of all he followed the God of Noah, and the Dragon covets them."

The Priest then turned his hands over, and upon the right palm, at the base of his thumb was a single serpent mark, freshly tattooed, raw, but not blue. "What would you have me do? This is the boy; shall I stain it as I have the others?"

Rosencross stared at the mark. What would it mean to share in the death of the Priest's son? And in the power of it? "I do not know Priest. I do not know."

There was a long silence. The candle flickered, and Rosencross quickly cupped his hands to protect it. The Priest retreated into the shadows.

Rosencross felt another presence take the Priest's place. He had felt it before, and he feared it. With an effort he turned his back slowly and walked up the stairs, thankful for the shred of candle light behind him.

For once the Priest had not salved his conscience, and he sought the faint shadow of life above. As he ascended the stone steps, a current of wind or maybe it was the Priest, snuffed the candle. Rosencross stiffened until the tavern sounds and the fire and the light within pushed the darkness back.

He paused a moment in the shadows.

In the tavern, six of his men ate and laughed amongst the tables. There were fourteen others whom he did not know. A number of them caressed shining swords, some were unraveling oiled leather wraps containing new battle-axes or chain mail. Men were grinning and joking and raising their weapons to the gift giver. His name rang out with each thanking—Lord Tostig.

Behind the bar, Elvodug and Flemup served drinks, and a little girl periodically poked her head from the kitchen with bowls of stew. Elvodug saw the Count in the shadows and nudged Flemup.

Rosencross sauntered forth. His shield-bearer, Jozibad, immediately rose from a chair near the door and stood close to his lord. It would have gone unnoticed except for his huge size and considerable mix of plate and chain armor. Rosencross's voice boomed, "Sir Tostig, I wish you all good fortune at the fair. Please receive my blessing." A hush. Men looked from Rosencross's powerful figure to Jozibad's even greater bulk and then at each other.

Elvodug began passing fourteen flagons of mead, and Flemup seven—his went only to the men that followed Rosencross. Most of Tostig's men shrugged their shoulders, but some were more guarded.

Rosenscross held his cup high. "Raise your cups that the gods will bless you and a blessing to King Strongbow." Then Tostig's men smiled and drank. Tostig did not raise his cup for the toast, nor to his lips, but walked across the room to stand before Rosencross.

"Our blessing also to you," Sir Tostig said, slightly nodding his head. "May I know your name; we will look forward to competing with you in the lists."

While the two men looked upon each other's person, a change in the room began to unfold. "Count Rosencross of Bannockburn," he said, returning the nod.

A few men staggered.

Sir Tostig raised his glass, but then lowered it again. "Please take no offense, but I cannot place either."

All around mugs clanked on table tops, some splashing their contents, while sluggish bodies sank into chairs.

"It is an island off Strongbow's coast, we came by ship." Rosencross drank deeply.

Tostig drank too. "I would like to know more —"

A Mug shattered upon the stones followed by a warrior who lurched forward as if to catch it. He hit the floor, tried to rise, and then fell silent.

Realization struck Sir Tostig as his men, and only his men, fell into chairs, across tables, or to the cobbled floor. He had drunk over half his cup.

He drew his sword and swung the blade towards Rosencross. Jozibad stepped in and parried the blow. Tostig tried to swing again, but only his arm moved, the sword slipped through his fingers and clanged upon the floor. He tottered forward, sank to his knees and fell at the Count's feet.

To Rosencross, the tavern suddenly felt oppressive, the air stifling. He stepped over Lord Tostig and out for some fresh air.

He called back through the open door, "Send them to the slavers."

Jozibad and the rest pulled the bodies down the circular stairs, past the dungeon, and loaded the carts.

Standing in the courtyard, Rosencross thought he heard a small voice speak the name of God. Walking towards the sound he looked through the open kitchen door. It was the little cook. Her back was to him as she worked at the stew pots. Then Elvodug peered into the kitchen from another entrance and called out, "No more bowls as of yet, child."

"Okay, uncle." She kept her body turned, her face down.

The Last Child

Count Rosencross felt the conscience pangs again, for he had often seen the boy, Thiery, as a companion to the little cook. It tore at his soul, rending a chasm within him, dark and void of all that is good, to which he felt he might be swallowed up. Then the girl began to sing one of her songs.

She was pure and melodious as a morning bird. The rending chasm within his breast retreated from the sound, and Rosencross felt relief, almost peace.

Entering through the side door, he slipped into a chair very near the child and watched her at the pots. She did not notice him as she sang, and measure by measure the demons of his past melted away. After a time, she stopped and bent her head to pray. Rosencross could not hear much, but he did hear his own name.

"Why do you speak of me?" Rosencross asked.

She dropped her ladle into the pot.

Suzie turned wide red eyes upon him.

"It's okay; I wish only to know what you have said concerning me."

"But you will not like it."

"Tell me, child, no harm will come to you."

"I will tell you, sir." And then she burst into tears and threw herself at his feet, wrapping her arms around his legs. Her body shook for long minutes, and for once Rosencross could think of nothing to do or say. He subsisted in a realm in which he was master—of court intrigue and battle—but this child's simple vulnerability sparked something within his breast, which he believed long dead, which in fact he had not remembered until now. He almost reached his hand to pat her head, almost.

Instead he waited.

"I am sorry, sir. But I am only a little girl. Please do not think that my heavenly Father has left me alone, because he has not, in fact he is quite by my side. But I have no earthly mother or father, and my uncle has taken me in, and while I try to love him, I see that he does not love me. And the only one who did love me, my brother, Thiery, has died." Rosencross stiffened.

This girl is the sister of the dead boy. Is she a daughter of the Priest then?

The Priest must not know, and if he found out, then she would not live long.

Suzie looked up at him with imploring eyes. "Oh, I would so like a family, a mother and a father who love each other, and they would love me too. My father would protect me and he would tell me about God just like fathers are supposed to. Doesn't that sound too wonderful?"

"Hmmm."

"And I'm afraid that my heart might break after seeing what I have seen this night." Again she broke into sobs.

"Child," Count Rosencross said, and this time he awkwardly patted the top of her head. "What is so terrible that you have seen?" But his face was ashen for he suspected her answer.

"It was you, sir, and Elvodug and Flemup, and the others ... you killed them. I saw you do it. It was very wrong, and it was much too much for a little girl to see. I am very sad inside." Rosencross left his hand hovering above the child as she rubbed her eyes. She stopped crying, but still she hid behind those tiny hands.

"They are not dead." His voice felt small.

At once her fingers spread, and one eye peeked between them. He looked away. "Oh, sir, I saw the wicked deed myself, and I do not like to accuse you of another sin, but I think ... oh dear, oh dear, this is a very bad day."

"Indeed you do unjustly accuse me of two wrongs. They are not dead. They are my property, my slaves, and I have told you the truth of it, not that I must answer to my cook."

"No, sir, you do not have to answer to me, only to Him."

"To whom?"

"To God. When you came in I was praying for you and you asked me what I was talking to Him about, and so I have told you."

"Hmmm ... well, in any event, the thing you saw was not so terrible after all."

Suzie smiled warmly, yet it made Rosencross uneasy. "I am glad you are not a murderer, and that I have not witnessed a murder. My Heavenly Father would not like that. It was still very unpleasant to see or even think about. So I will try not to. But at least you are just a man-stealer and a deceiver, so perhaps your heart is not so hardened that you will not open it up to Him, and now I will know what to pray for. I will pray that you will let those men go, and tell them you are sorry."

"Hmmm."

Suzie moved to a chair, closed her eyes, and began to pray. As Rosencross stole from the chamber, the last thing he heard was, "Oh please, please, please set those nice men free." He glanced back and could see that her request was directed heavenward, and not at him.

Suzie's Protector

Count Rosencross sat at the bar. Jozibad, covered in armor, kept his place at the door—watching the room, watching the patrons, watching his master.

Rosencross saw the fear in Flemup and Elvodug as they served tables and glanced towards himself and Jozibad. This was something new that they couldn't understand. Why was the Count drinking at the bar in the middle of the day? The thought caused Rosencross to smirk over his drink.

It was past noon, and he hadn't eaten. The drink felt warm in his belly, when suddenly the little face of Suzie peeked out from the kitchen. Her eyebrows raised, there was a trace of a smile, and then she was gone. Rosencross, for the first time in a very long time felt something stir in his heart—care, protection, perhaps father-like love. He could not tell. But he felt as if he must keep her safe, even if it meant that she would be gone.

If he sent her away, her songs no longer would salve his conscience, but at least she would be protected from the Priest. Rosencross glared at the pretend uncles as they worked the bar and served food. He laughed inwardly at their anxiety.

Perhaps his Priest would not know the care he felt for the child. Perhaps the jealousy of the Dragon would not be revealed. But since his heart was moved for the girl, and he had been away long, he worried over the consequence. The Priest must be met with soon, or he would know something was amiss. He always knew.

So thinking, he prepared to leave, calling upon the Dragon for strength. But then Suzie appeared with a plate of specially prepared delicacies. Her large eyes looked upon him with trust, so that he had to look away, knowing the evil in his heart.

"I don't think you have eaten lunch today, so I made you something," Suzie said, smiling. "You have been so kind to let me spend time with the animals and Oded, and with you, I feel like I might burst with happiness. Thank you."

Rosencross smiled at her, then saw Flemup minding the conversation and scowled him from the room. Suddenly he proposed an idea. "I have decided that you are well suited to the keeping of the animals, and to helping Oded with them. Would you like to be his helper? Mornings in the kitchen, and the rest of the day would be yours."

"Oh, oh, oh." Suzie clapped her little hands, and trembled. "I would like that very much!" But then her face saddened. "I don't think my uncles will like it."

"I am master here. They will like whatever I tell them. It is settled then. Run out and tell Oded. I will deal with your uncles." Suzie disappeared into the courtyard. Her excited calls for Oded resonated back through the Inn.

Rosencross stood. He looked towards the dark stairwell, took a deep breath, and set out to find his Priest.

The first level below the Inn was lit by candles. It was built from a mixture of stone and wood. Several red-robed priests sat at table playing cards. Rosencross barely gave them a second look, knowing that his Priest would not be among them.

The stairs again turned to stone, and he proceeded to their last rendezvous. As he approached, a faint light—candle or oil lamp, he could not tell—fluttered and descended below him, one or two flights beyond his reach. Was it the Priest? Where was he being led? He continued, but whenever he hurried the glow accelerated, and when he slowed it slowed, so that always, his foot rested upon stones obscured in darkness before he could reach them.

Soon the air changed, heavy with damp, and the stairs became uneven and wet. "Priest," he called. "I weary of this descent, taunt me no longer."

"You avoid me of late," his shrill voice called back. "I think you hide a secret from me, and I would know what it is. My servants tell me that you listen to the songs of Noah's God from that little cook."

"You forget yourself. I don't do your bidding."

There was silence. The light began to flicker, and then it grew darker. The Priest was moving again. As Rosencross came around the next bend in the circular stairs, a large passage opened on the left. He had not been this low before. It made him uneasy, and he decided that he would not come again without Jozibad.

The passage widened into a chamber. Oil lamps were lit upon the walls, and a twenty foot wide river passed through. A stone bridge crossed the river to a raised bed of rock where an immense metal door was set into the cave wall.

The Priest finished lighting the lamps. "Do not get too close to the water. I sent two priests on a boat to explore downstream, but they did not come back. We have seen the river stir in strange ways. And we've been leaving ... things ... tied up, and when we return they've been consumed."

"And the door?" Rosencross asked.

"One of the gates to Tump Barrows. It's not been given for free passage, permission must be granted in order to use it. Two Dwarves came to dinner last night, but they did not come through the front door, and so we are fairly certain that they came this way. There are many passages, so we can't be sure."

"Where are they now?"

"We think they are beyond that door. Possibly they are the gate-keepers. I have priests hidden along the stairs. They watched you. They watch everyone who comes and goes. When they come to eat again, we will be ready."

"Hmmm ... have you tried the gate?"

"Some, it won't open."

Rosencross was annoyed—so much happening without his being informed. He would watch these priests more carefully from now on.

"Are you finished with me, Count?" The Priest asked. Was there a double meaning in his words? Could he sense that much?

"For now," Rosencross said. "But let me know the moment you learn anything." He had trouble keeping the edge from his voice.

The Priest smiled, but he looked more like a grinning hyenae, lingering over a meal. "We need a sacrifice. This place would do very well. The Dragon summons and the games begin soon. Perhaps one of the believers in Noah's God would be best."

"Perhaps, but I'd best return. I've things to do." Rosencross turned away, taking a lamp from the wall. The Priest began extinguishing the remaining lamps.

As Rosencross turned to ascend the steps, the last of the lamps went out. His light was not enough to keep back all the darkness. "Do you come up Priest?"

From the other side of the river, a voice echoed, but nothing could be seen. "No, Count, I'll pray here awhile."

Rosencross abruptly left and began his ascent until he knew no light could reach the chamber from where he had left the Priest. Then leaving his lamp upon the stairs he returned—slow, deliberate steps to the chamber's entrance, waiting to see if the Priest would light a lamp, or if he truly steeped himself in the blackness.

Thirty minutes passed. The dark was stifling and oppressive, especially as his own imaginations conspired
against him. He thought he heard an occasional sound
from within, but no light. Then there was a slight splash
of water, and something scraped along the stones. It
seemed to move in his direction. What serpent or beast
could it be? Rosencross hurried from the spot, grabbed
his lamp and climbed from the depths.

It was settled then. He would hear one more song
and then send her away. Now that Thiery was dead,
there were only two within their expedition who served
Noah's God. Oded the Bear and Suzie. The Priest, he
knew, would choose the girl.

The Stranger

The moment Thiery saw the blade reflecting firelight, and a white grimace in the shadows, he put his escape into effect. Oded said always be aware of how best to advance and more importantly how best to retreat. So Thiery pushed himself away from the rock face and fell to the cave floor, cushioned by sleeping skins he had bundled below.

He collapsed and rolled to save his feet and ankles from the fall. In one motion he rose and picked up the bow, where six arrows lay waiting. He nocked one and drew back.

His retreat was perfectly executed, except for one thing. Horatio thought it was a game. His paws danced, he spun in circles, and bounded into the air. Then as Thiery stood rigid with bow in hand, Horatio lowered his head, crouched, and pounced. Thiery released as he fell and the arrow sped into the upper cave, splintering against the rock. He scrambled to his feet as fear heated his belly in knots. Another arrow lay broken at his feet, trampled. Only four left.

"Ssssst," Thiery commanded as he thrust his cupped hand into Horatio's neck: a toothless bite. Horatio's ears fell flat and he immediately ceased his play. Thiery recovered the bow and nocked another arrow. But nothing moved. Minutes passed and the only sounds came from the crackling fire, and an occasional bird calling from the forest without.

Thiery glanced at Horatio, whose head cocked to the side. Horatio should have been keenly aware of danger. But the wolf sat still and relaxed, never bothering to look towards the upper cave.

Thiery looked up again, and called into the darkness. "What do you want?" His voice was startling after the silence.

There was no response. No head or weapon appeared over the edge.

"Bloody and deceitful men won't live out half their days," Thiery called out into the hidden places.

He could leave the cave, but there were only a few hours of daylight left, hardly enough time to find and effect a secure camp. Moreover he was not certain that the man was an enemy, maybe he was wounded or sick. And how had he gotten there? Thiery suddenly felt a surging desire for fellowship. But for now, he must assume the worst: a naked blade draws blood.

There had been light coming from the upper cave. In the seconds before he jumped, Thiery had gathered a vague picture of its size and direction. Cautiously, he put the rest of his wood and an ample pile of leaves upon the fire, and withdrew to the forest.

Forty feet up, smoke wafted from the hillside. Thiery had not yet explored the rocky terrain rising up over the river, so he climbed, searching for a perch from which he could observe the cave mouth below. Evergreen bushes and trees speckled the rise, aiding the ascent.

Boyish excitement for any climb—heightened by uncertainty of the stranger—coursed adventure through Thiery's soul. Furthermore, he had the beginnings of an idea gathering shape as he made his way towards the smoke. The chimney outlet, a symmetrical hole in the rock, was a hand's span in diameter, and Thiery stuffed it shut with his flint pouch.

Unless there were other passages that the smoke could escape from, the swordsman would have to come out, and then Thiery could decide better what to do. Stay or flee. The day's activities were having their effects on his fatigued and recovering body, so he hoped he could stay.

Intent on the cave entrance below, Thiery failed to notice the hint of change behind. A half hour passed and still no one had appeared, when the thought struck Thiery that he might have suffocated the stranger.

Panicked, he turned to remove the pouch, but his hand poised undecided. For, looking behind him, he saw that the smoke had found another way out. It streamed from a ledge not far away. So absorbed had he been with the expected, he had forgotten to be wary of the unexpected.

He scrambled to the smoking ledge. It ran for about fifteen feet in length and five feet deep, with a sheer cliff face rising from it. Billowing white enshrouded the farthest point, which was tucked into the rocky cliff. As the smoke eddied about the rocks, small gusts of wind, rising up from the valley, would burst through, revealing planed wood and then bands of metal, only to disappear again in a sheet of smoke. A door to the upper cave!

Returning to his pouch, Thiery removed it—hot smoke burst forth—ducking away, he took up his new post on the ledge, Horatio at his side. Slowly, the air cleared and a small door, only five feet tall appeared.

Carved into the wood, was written 'God's peace upon all who enter.'

"Oh boy," Thiery said. "I've not been exactly peaceful." Some vines grew across the corner, and the base had no discernable groove, just dirt and moss. "Horatio, I don't think this door's been used for a while. Maybe he's escaped the smoke by another passage." But that was not to be.

The door was skillfully constructed, and it soon swung outward with only slight protest. Light feathered the chamber revealing a simple wood table and two chairs. Hanging above it, suspended from the cave ceiling was an oil lamp chandelier.

Thiery stepped into the chamber, bow ready, and marked the shadowy form of the stranger thirty feet away to the right. He was sitting against the rocks just where Thiery had left him.

Thiery scraped his boot along the cave floor. Still the man did not move. So he waited in the entrance for his eyes to fully adjust, and let Horatio enter ahead of him. Again, the wolf showed no signs of fear, disappearing into blackness off to the left. His padded feet softly echoed.

Keeping the stranger in sight, Thiery lit the lamps and gasped. Everywhere he turned some unexpected sight met him.

The table was covered with vellum skins; there were beautifully scripted words and drawings. And he could read them—they were not babbled—but written in his own tongue. Whoever the stranger was, he came from the same ancestor, and they spoke the same language. Thiery could hardly wait to pore over the documents.

Splattered across the cave walls were paintings of dragons and beasts of all sorts. In the far corner where Horatio had gone, stood clay pots, rope, and arrows ... Thiery could have suffered greatly increased hardship without more arrows. Thiery's eyes were wet as he thought of God's provision. But most of all, he was thankful that he had not killed the stranger. He was certainly dead, but it was not Thiery's smoke that had done it.

Leather armor imbedded with iron plates hung loose upon the stranger's bones. The white skull and hand were limp and stark against the flickering light. The sword grip rested upon his thigh, and the tip hovered in the air because of a stone placed further back along the weapon's length. It was beautifully crafted, and Thiery would take it, but he was not quite ready to disturb the stranger. There was still much to discover, and night was coming quick.

Thiery turned to look at Horatio and realized his ears were peaked and his head tilted. A moment later and Thiery heard the whistle too. He knew that sound. It was the timing for the rowers.

They would see the smoke.

Thiery ran for the chimney and once again plugged it with his pouch. It would take some time for the smoke to build and push its way out the door; by then it would be dark enough and the fire would be out.

As he slid and tumbled down the hillside he could hear the whistle more clearly, and men's voices too. Running inside the cave he scattered the fire, scooping dirt upon the larger pieces, and then he climbed the rock face, past the bony swordsman, and back out onto the ledge above the river.

There, in the waning light he watched the boat with fourteen oarsman glide to the river's edge below. They were chained to the benches. And standing upon the deck he saw a half score of Count Rosencross' warriors. Horatio growled and the hair bristled along his back.

A voice called out. "We'll camp here. Unchain seven slaves for each half of the night." It was Igi Forkbeard. But Thiery didn't recognize any of the rowers, and he had often watched the camp slaves at work. These were all new. By the look of them, their spirits would be hard to break. But that was Forkbeard's specialty.

Another warrior spoke then. "They're still weak, we'll not have any trouble from them tonight."

"It doesn't matter," Forkbeard said. "That lord there, he follows the God of Noah, and I'll not take chances with them." The man in question raised his head slowly, his eyes were lined and blood shot.

Some of the warriors smirked. Igi Forkbeard leapt to his feet and stared down at his men. He was a head and shoulders taller than the biggest of them: some said he was a son of the giant Oddhelm. He walked over to where the slaves sat, and drew his sword above the one he called a lord. "I'm not afraid of men, and I know that some of you mock Noah's God, but I sat at the feet of Japeth when I was a boy, and heard him speak of the flood, and of the world before it. He said they were wicked continually, and I for one will not tempt the God that destroyed the earth. I follow Marduk just as you, but to tempt the gods is foolish."

Igi's speech had its effects. The men no longer smiled. They moved further from the captive lord, and many looked up at the moon and the first stars appearing.

"Look!" A warrior pointed at some black clouds mounting over the tops of the trees.

Thiery watched it all and sat in thought as the men prepared food and lit a fire. "Oh, Lord," Thiery prayed, "he testifies of you without knowing you. Please show me my way, a lamp unto my feet and a light unto my path."

Soon their fire was blazing, and the moon no longer shone, so that the firelight made the blackness over the water and along the hills and the woods, advance and retreat like a thousand striking serpents. The pale faces of the seven slaves, left upon the boat appeared and then disappeared from the firelight's effects. And it was into this circle of light and dark that Thiery suddenly emerged, a cloth bundle under his arm, and a white wolf at his side.

Warriors dropped food, as some turned or rose from the ground; swords and battle-axes menaced the air. A few moved forward, and then as the firelight declared Thiery's face, it was as if God stopped time. Nothing moved or sounded but the fire. Not a creak of armor. And then a hushed talk swept towards Thiery's ears.

"I know it's true," Thiery said. "That you are a brave man Igi Forkbeard, not because I have heard it from your own lips, but from the lips of others. Even the bards have mentioned you in their songs, but what you fear, and rightly so, is no living man."

Weaponless hands rubbed amulets or made the sign of the cross—the sign of Tammuz. One warrior wielding a sword in each hand crossed the blades before him.

Igi Forkbeard paled. "Do you come back from the dead for blessings or cursings?"

Thiery thought back to the day he entered his tent, with the whole army watching, and then he remembered the voice of his father and Count Rosencross speaking of his death. These men thought he was an apparition, a spirit.

"I am as one who has touched the veil, but I am real. The Most High God has chosen to keep me for another day. I came down here to tell you more of the One you rightly fear: God, the Creator, the Judge, and the Redeemer of souls. I came to ask for the freedom of this lord and his men because you testified that he calls upon the God of Noah. And I came to warn you." He tossed the cloth bundle at the feet of the captive lord. Slowly, the man retrieved it and felt inside without removing its cover.

Igi scowled at the action but did not intercede. "They are not mine to set free. I only obey the Count's orders. If your god wants them then why does he not just do it himself? If they try to leave by natural means then we will stop them or cut them down. But if supernatural then what can man do? If your god will take them, then we will bow before him as he does so. And I would like to *see* him, for I understand that he does not allow images to be made of himself."

"I cannot make Him appear," Thiery replied. "But you will bow before Him one day. Besides this, you are without excuse, Igi Forkbeard. You hold the truth of God in unrighteousness. You ask to see, but he has already shown you. The invisible things of Him from the creation of the world are clearly seen, being understood by the things that are made, even his eternal power and Godhead. Just look at the Earth suspended in the Heavens. You can see His handiwork everywhere. Just now your men looked at the clouds darkening the stars and they feared the flood that God might send. But He has placed the rainbow in the sky as a promise to us that He'll not destroy us with water ever again. Yet God's wrath is against ungodliness and unrighteousness, and He will not wink at it forever. Today is the day of salvation for those who will turn fully to Him."

"But I can see the gods of Marduk, and Baal, and others." Igi pointed to an idol by the fire.

"You are God's creation, and He designed man to know Him, but when they knew God, they glorified him not as God, neither were thankful; but became vain in their imaginations, and their foolish heart was darkened. Professing themselves to be wise, they became fools, and changed the glory of the uncorruptible God into an image made like to corruptible man, and to birds, and fourfooted beasts, and creeping things. Wherefore God also gave them up to uncleanness through the lusts of their own hearts, to dishonour their own bodies between themselves: Who changed the truth of God into a lie, and worshipped and served the creature more than the Creator. These gods you see and worship are just dead images that can do nothing of themselves."

There was angry muttering among the men. Then Thiery noticed that the moon was shining again, and some of the trees behind the warriors were bent and moving unnaturally. "Listen, quickly!" Thiery cried. "You may not see another day. For the past two nights, a creature has hunted this glen, and it seems to me that he draws close again. If you die tonight, will you find yourself with Hell compassed about you? Or will you turn from your false gods and serve the Most High?"

"Your speech is strange —"

"Sir," One of the warriors called out, pointing his sword toward the woods at their back. "I heard something." No one spoke or moved. The forest was quiet, too much so. "I think I hear breathing."

Then what looked like a great mass of tangled trees shifted a few feet to the side, just beyond the firelight.

Men spun round with shields raised, and then closed ranks to make a shield wall. The captive lord drew the sword Thiery had given him, and edged towards the boat with his men, unnoticed by Igi Forkbeard.

Then the creature was among them, and the shield wall burst as if it were made of children's play things. The wave of battle instantly pressed upon Thiery as the creature's huge mouth swung, and its tail knocked men lifeless to the earth, and its claws sliced through weapons, armor and flesh alike.

Thiery and Horatio fled up the side of the hill. Drawing his bow, he stood upon the ledge and fired his last four arrows into the beast before rushing into the upper cave for more.

Guest

Thiery's hands shook as he tried to light the lamp. The sounds outside were fierce, and the thought of men dying, for that was surely happening, was causing an ache to tighten in his chest. "Oh please, Lord, let some live."

Minutes passed before he got the lamp lit and he could see the cave once more. There was the quiver. Catching up the arrows he nocked one and cautiously slipped out onto the ledge. But it was already over.

The boat was no longer anchored at the shore.

The natural sounds of the night returned.

The soldiers lay strewn about the glen, broken and twisted in the moonlight. Then one of them stirred, and pulled himself to his knees. It was the unmistakable bulk of Igi Forkbeard. He went to one and then another of his fallen men, speaking their names and gently touching their pallid skin. Thiery made his way down beside him.

Forkbeard didn't seem to notice him, but he did speak. "All of them." And Thiery knew that they were all dead. Yet God had answered his prayer. One man still stood before him, and all the slaves seemed to have escaped.

"I'm sorry, sir," Thiery said, "that you've lost your friends."

"Friends?" Igi Forkbeard spun round, and balled his fingers into two massive fists. "These were not my friends. I have none, and I haven't need of any." A tear vanished into his beard.

"No friends? That's awful. I'm not sure where my friends are, though I have been longing for them." Thiery held out his hand. "Maybe you and I could be friends?"

Igi did not answer. He looked towards the river, then into the woods where the creature had come from, and again at his men. The fire lay scattered in small bits around the glen.

Thiery let his arm fall awkwardly, but he was not ready to give up. "I have a safe place to sleep not far from here, and you're welcome to join me. The creature might come back." Thiery walked to the edge of the clearing, and started to climb.

Igi Forkbeard didn't follow.

Thiery called back to him. "It's right up this hill. I'll cook something, and I'll make enough for you. Come when you're ready."

In a half hour some fish were broiling over coals. Thiery rubbed them with dried herbs found within the cave. If he could only get Igi close enough to smell the aroma, he might have a guest. Still he waited. Then, remembering the difficult climb and the concealed door, Thiery took up a lamp and set it out on the ledge. "If it be your will, please send him here, Lord."

The table in the center of the cave was still covered with vellum and parchment scrolls. Thiery lovingly gathered them and set them aside for later. He glanced over some of the titles: *A Ranger's Bestiary*, *The Record of Noah's Flood*, *Regional Caves and the Dwarven Brotherhood*, *The Book of Job* ... and then there was a knock at his door.

Thiery ran to let him in, suddenly wondering if someone as large as Igi Forkbeard could fit through such a small portal. He swung the door open, and Igi's wide hand reached inside passing over the lamp from without. Both were wet with rain.

Next, weapons and armor were handed through, and Thiery struggled to place them and grab some more, until a heap of glistening swords, battle-axes, gauntlets and the like, occasionally dented or smeared with blood, were collected safely within. Finally, Igi Forkbeard's head appeared, as he wriggled through the doorway on all fours with his broad armored shoulders angled and scraping along the beams.

Within the cave he stretched almost to his full height. His nostrils flared, sniffing and turning his head slightly, and then sniffing again. "How is it that you have come back from the dead? Are you flesh or spirit?" His eyes jumped from Thiery to the cooked fish.

"I'm flesh, and while I came close to death, I didn't die. When I came out of the sick tent on my own two feet, the camp was gone."

"You are the one called Thiery, yes? The one who trained under Oded?"

"Yes."

"There were rumors also that you had not been truly sick, but that you were murdered. That is why my men and I thought you were a spirit, one of vengeance. Yet you saved me?"

"I only warned you, and too late."

"No. I challenged your God to take away the slaves if He wanted them, and He sent that great dragon beast into our camp and freed them. And then your arrows, for I saw the bow upon your back, kept me alive."

"How do you mean, sir?" Thiery asked.

"In seconds I found myself pinned beneath the creature, and one of its claws pressed upon my breastplate. The tip pierced through and just into my skin. It could have nailed me to the earth, but it paused and looked into my eyes." As Igi Forkbeard spoke, his hand played at the hole in his armor, a dark red stain was visible beneath.

"I called to your God then. The dragon's mouth opened with row upon row of teeth, and its tongue was like a snake. At that moment, an arrow, your arrow, was suddenly stuck in that snake of a tongue. It released its grip upon me and I rolled free, only to be knocked down, and pitted to the earth. Again the creature had me, and again it paused, giving me space to ask your God to save me. Then another of your arrows appeared where its eye had just been. In a rage it smashed and cut and chomped among us, and then it was gone."

They both sat in silence. Igi stared at the young Thiery, guarded.

"Praise him for his mighty acts," Thiery proclaimed boldly. "You said that you asked God to save you. Was it just a momentary thing, or are you truly calling upon the God of Noah now?"

More silence.

"You'll not live forever, and then it will be too late, for it is appointed unto man once to die, and then the judgment."

"Enough!" Igi Forkbeard's fist crashed upon the table. "We will eat, not talk, and then I will speak."

Thiery retrieved the fish and laid it before them. He began to say something and then stopped.

Igi grinned. "Good, you learn quick."

Thiery closed his eyes. "Thank you, God, for this food before us. Thank you for sparing my friend from death, please soften his prideful heart. How long a person will refuse to humble themselves before you, only you know. Thank you that if he shall humble himself, and pray, and seek your face, and turn from his wicked ways, then you will hear from heaven, and forgive his sin, and you will be his God."

Thiery opened his eyes. Igi wore a frown; bits of fish were clasped between his fingers, hovering before his mouth.

Igi Forkbeard stayed with Thiery for two days, asking about the God of Noah. Thiery read to him from the book of Job and did his best to rightly represent God accurately. But Igi struggled with ties to Marduk and the gods of his fathers, while Thiery left no room for a man to sit upon the fence. Many times Igi's fiery temper would reverberate through the cave.

Twice the sturdy table lay legless upon the floor from the pounding of fists, and twice Thiery repaired the damage, smiling gently, with no trace of reproof. Horatio's wolf head would lift and cock to the side at these antics, but seeing Thiery's calm manner, he would again lay with his nose between his paws, eyes and mouth seeming to smile.

Red in the face, Igi suddenly noticed the wolf. "You're both crazy, even your dog doesn't get riled, and he mocks me with that grin."

On one such occasion, Igi cried out "How do I know this is a true story? Where is this land of Uz anyway? I've never heard of it."

"Do you mean to say that you will not believe in God because you have no proof that Job is a real person? Do you believe that I am real?"

"Of course I do, you crazy boy. I can see you with my own eyes."

"Yes, but before you saw me, would you take another's word for my existence? Or, upon hearing my name would you instantly interrupt with an accusation that I was a figment of their imagination, and that you would not believe another word until proof was forthcoming?"

"That is ridiculous. Why would I even care to question?"

"So then why do you question Job?"

"Because you say that I cannot follow Noah's and Job's God at the same time as I follow my own which have served me well. To follow your God then I must give up much, and I would have proof that he is the only god, as you say. Not only this, but he did not serve Job well, but instead he let terrible evil come upon him. What do you say now youngling? I think I have you, yes?" Igi Forkbeard leaned back with his arms crossed upon his barrel of a chest, smiling.

As Thiery thought of what to say, Igi added, "I am ready to give homage to your god, don't misunderstand, for you have shown me with your bow that he is one whom I should regard, but I have lived through forty years of battle and my gods have brought me through till now. Would you have me disown them?"

"Yes, indeed, sir. For there is but one God, and Job was served as his God saw fit. As he said to his wife 'shall we receive good at the hand of God, and shall we not receive evil?' and also 'naked came I out of my mother's womb, and naked shall I return thither: the LORD gave, and the LORD hath taken away; blessed be the name of the LORD.' You want your gods because of what you believe they will do for you, and so you contemplate the God of Noah for the same reason. And what He will give you is worth more than anything in this life. He will give you eternal life. But *He* is God, and *He* is who we are to serve and think about, not ourselves. Even Job struggled with his lot, and wanted to bring his case before God. As Job said, to 'find Him, that I might come even to his seat! I would order my cause before him, and fill my mouth with arguments. I would know the words which he would answer me, and understand what he would say unto me.'"

"Yes, and I think it fair," Igi said. "If Job was his best follower, then why not have an answer?"

"To ask for an answer, God allows, but not that God should be placed upon trial by one of *His* creation, and an answer be demanded of Him."

"But then Job has a right to go to another god, if there is no answer or he does not like what he hears." Igi Forkbeard laughed, then added, "Aha then, my case is a good one, I think I have got you."

"Sir, you but argue with mankind, and I'm just a boy. Why not instead, hear the answer of your Creator. And yes, He has allowed you to choose eternal Hell with your false demon gods if you like, but He calls you to join Him." Thiery began turning through the rolled sheepskin parchments until he came upon the passage he required.

Igi grumbled under his breath as he waited. "False demon gods. Have a care, or who knows as what they'll do to you, young Thiery."

"Then the Lord answered," Thiery read, and then paused to look into Igi's dark stare. "The Lord answered Job out of the whirlwind, and said, who is this that darkeneth counsel by words without knowledge?"

Igi slammed his fist upon the table. "Does it really say that? Are you trying to tell me I have no knowledge?"

"It really says it. Shall I continue?"

"Just don't anger me."

"It says, 'Gird up now thy loins like a man; for I will demand of thee, and answer thou me. Where wast thou when I laid the foundations of the earth? Declare, if thou hast understanding.'"

"How could I know such a thing? Skip to the part where your God answers my question. Why did Noah's God treat his best follower so badly?"

"Okay, how about this." Again Thiery read from the parchment. "Hast thou entered into the springs of the sea? Or hast thou walked in the search of the depth?"

"That is not an answer; I think you are trying to make me mad. How can I walk in the depth of the sea? And springs are on land, not in water."

Thiery smiled gently and continued to read aloud. "Have the gates of death been opened unto thee? Or hast thou seen the doors of the shadow of death?"

At this, Igi Forkbeard looked pale, and he glanced toward the open door where the day-light shone, then he squinted into the recesses of the cave, and towards the sitting skeleton, and then back at Thiery. He raised a spoon from the table and prodded Thiery's hand, as if to be certain that it was flesh and not spirit.

"Did you make that up? Who would willingly enter the gates of ..." Igi's voice dropped to a whisper. "I do not like to say it."

"It is written here, as is this, 'Where is the way where light dwelleth? And as for darkness, where is the place thereof?' What do you say to that one, sir? Light does indeed have a way, and darkness a place. Light is always traveling, and moving through, and opening up or exposing the place of darkness. When light stops moving there is darkness. Who, but God, knows how it all works?"

"You make my head ache. This is a very long answer to my question; in fact it seems no answer at all."

Again Thiery bent over the parchment. "By what way is the light parted, which scattereth the east wind upon the earth?"

"Ha, that is ridiculous. Light does not cause the wind."

"You say so with such surety. You must then know what causes the wind."

"Me?" Igi rubbed at his square jaw. "Well, of course I do not."

"How do you know then that wind is not caused by light? You are aware that there is a lower entrance to this cave that borders upon the cool forest below. At that place the sun-light does not shine. Have you then noticed what occurs as the sun-light warms the ledge that our front door exits on?" Thiery paused, but when the only answer forthcoming was gritting teeth, he said, "There is a great cool wind that blows from within the cave and into the open air. I do not know why, but it does seem that the light from the sun is what caused this wind. So, why not on a much grander scale?"

Scores of such questions, from the book of Job, were put to Igi Forkbeard, of the great dragons behemoth and leviathan and other animals of God's creation, of rain, snow, ice and rivers, of the stars of heaven, and much more—things that he understood not, things too wonderful to know. And finally it was too much to bear. Igi's frame swelled and raged. And the table again lay broken upon the floor. He retreated through the cave door, squeezing himself into the day, as he called back, "You did not answer my question, and you have angered me, just as I carefully forbade you. I shall stay here no more."

Thiery called after him, "But all those questions, they are the answer God gives."

A short while later Igi Forkbeard's face appeared in the door. "I owe you two debts. You saved my life twice. I will repay one of those debts now. The armor and gold from my fallen men is yours to do with as you like, it is worth much. I also give you information. It is better if Count Rosencross and his priests do not know you are alive, for if they find out, I am sure that you will not be alive long. I will not tell them. Until the fair is over at least, they are masters of the Hilltop Inn. The highway passes along its gate only a quarter days walk from here, but this river also flows close by it. Most of the Count's army is hid within a grotto along its banks. But Oded stays at the Inn's stables with the animals. Oded was never sick, and he has returned suspicious, but he thinks you dead. This, I think, repays my first debt." Then he was gone, and Thiery was alone with Horatio and his thoughts.

Duty

Lord McDougal crouched beside Fergus Leatherhead and their new companion, Gimcrack. The forest covered them in shadows. A squirrel scampered through the branches building a nest high above them. Every few minutes it launched acorn missiles in their direction.

"We could arrive at a late hour," Fergus offered, "keep our travel cloaks pulled tight, and ask for food to be brought up to our room. Just in case witch Esla's prophecy is in fact a threat, or worse yet, a plot."

"Your counsel is good; we will follow it," McDougal said as he reached to catch a falling acorn.

The Hilltop Inn stretched out before them, a few guards walked the walls, and an occasional traveler arrived for dinner, or a room.

Just before dark, the courtyard gate swung wide. From a spot unseen, two immense figures ambled quietly from the woods.

The first was a fourteen foot grizzly, walking erect, with a young girl clinging to its back. She sat upon some kind of saddle or harness.

Following close, with one hand outstretched behind the girl, was a giant, or perhaps the son of a giant, for he only neared a height of nine feet. His arms and legs were encased in a combination of plate armor and chain mail, while from his torso hung a leather tunic reaching to his knees. A round shield was strapped upon his back, and in one hand he carried what looked like a sizeable metal chest impaled upon a fat table leg, but upon further scrutiny, it could be seen to be a great, rectangular, war hammer.

He gave a command and the bear dropped to all fours. The girl's faint giggle traveled on the breeze. Then she leapt from the saddle and into the giant's arms hugging him about his neck. In a moment they disappeared beyond the gate. While the scene unfolded, Fergus noted the attentive care of the giant man and knew what McDougal would say next.

"He seems a noble fellow, and she a charming girl. I like them," McDougal said, smiling. "Perhaps we should arrange a meeting."

"That is Oded, the one they call the Bear, friend to the boy," Gimcrack whispered, suddenly perspiring. "And the girl is Suzie, cook's helper, and also a friend of the boy. I can't go in there, if Oded is here, then Count Rosencross and the priests must be too. When they see that I live … oh, I can't go in there."

Fergus and McDougal exchanged glances.

"God is so very good," McDougal said, pointedly. "I only longed for a bed and cooked food, but now He has led us onto the trail of young Thiery. Mayhap we will yet find him tonight." He paused to study Gimcrack's frightened form.

"Tell me, Gimcrack," McDougal asked, "are you my man?"

"Yes, my Lord."

"Do you follow me?"

"Yes, my Lord."

"Do you obey me?"

"Yes, my Lord."

"Good, if you do those things, then you do your duty, and you are found a faithful follower. You will be honored as a man of integrity.

"What if I tell you to go in there with Fergus and myself?" McDougal pointed towards the Inn.

Gimcrack's neck snapped towards the Hilltop Inn, his eyes were wide, and slowly he turned back towards McDougal. Just before they looked face to face, Gimcrack dropped his gaze and rubbed his fingers along the back of his knuckles. His eye was twitching again.

The Squirrel dropped an acorn. It bounced off Gimcrack's shoulder. He flinched.

"Let me tell you a story about my brother, Theodoro," McDougal said. "He was fifteen at the time, four years older than I was. Fergus and I followed him whenever we could. He and my father, they were our heroes.

"One day my brother was hunting our lands. As he entered a pass to the valley, my father burst forth from the rocky slope, sword drawn.

"'Theodoro,' Father called. 'Giants. If they come this way, you keep the pass. They could be here in twenty minutes.'

"Theodoro climbed a ledge, and gathered large stones to throw upon the invaders. He had twelve arrows and his sword. No food and little water.

"My father ran down the slopes, and just as he was out of sight from my brother, a poisonous serpent bit father in the leg. Fergus and I found him unconscious, not far from the castle. We built a makeshift litter and dragged him home. The nights were cold. For two days it rained, and still father laid unconscious, and no one knew what had become of Theodoro. On the fourth day father awoke, and asked for my brother.

"Discovering what had transpired, we rode out and found him still keeping the pass. There were no giants. Father had been testing Theodoro, as was his manner. And my brother was faithful to his charge.

"He did not leave his post for food or water, but waited for the enemy. He did not leave to escape the rain or bitter nights. His father had given a command, and he would not let him down, nor bring dishonor to his name. He was faithful, even unto death."

"Do you mean to say," Gimcrack asked, wide eyed, "that your brother died?"

"He did."

There were tears in McDougal's eyes, yet he was smiling, as he always did when he told this tale. Fergus had to grind his teeth exceedingly hard, and not look upon his lord, for that strange sensation in his eyes and nose was back, threatening to knock a piece from his stoic armor.

"While my brother waited upon those rocks, he left us a heritage to give to our children and to our children's children. With his dagger, he carved these words, 'Fear God, and keep His commandments.' And upon another stone he inscribed, 'Thy father's commandment, when thou goest, it shall lead thee; when thou sleepest, it shall keep thee; and when thou awakest, it shall talk with thee.'"

Gimcrack looked away again.

Fergus sighed.

"It's almost dark," McDougal said. "Fergus and I will sleep in the Inn. Tomorrow morning we'll bring you some breakfast. I don't know how long it will take to find the boy or at least word of him. We may have to stay two nights, so make yourself as comfortable as you can. The larger predators probably won't hunt this close to the Inn, but you might want to find a stout tree to sleep in. Think upon your duty. If I had asked you to join us tonight, would you have come?" He then patted Gimcrack upon the back, prayed a blessing upon him, and walked to the oaken doors of the Hilltop Inn.

Fergus followed, proud of his lord. And McDougal's walk—it was once again most beautiful to behold.

Gimcrack watched until the doors closed. He sat in the stillness of dusk.

Opening a canister, he withdrew a map, cut a small scrap of vellum, and leaned over it in the waning light. He scribbled some words, then, gathering some acorns, he laid them upon the note and fled into the night.

The squirrel chattered in triumph, and descended to gather. Among its spoils was a piece of vellum.

The Unconscious Torturer

As they shut the door behind them, the waning light outside matched the muted light within. The tavern was lit by sconces at the bar, a small fire in the hearth, and long tapered candles at each table.

The room was nearly full with bodies. A few tables only, were vacant. Voices rose and fell. It was warm.

Sitting on a bench behind the door, and leaning against the wall, a heavily armored man looked up. His plate mail was highly polished, reflecting every illumination, so that he shimmered, seeming to move while perfectly still.

Fergus could sense the man's hollow stare—though it was hidden within a snake-plumed helm—follow them into the room. It was difficult to turn his back on the warrior.

They headed towards the barkeeper, a distance of thirty or so feet. They would pass five tables crowded with guests, and one empty. Many of the spaces between tables were only a couple hand spans apart—most difficult to navigate while weighed down with traveling gear. Worse yet, were the many pairs of eyes fastened on the two hooded strangers.

Fergus' mouth was dry. McDougal's hands suddenly seemed like two foreign body parts, tripping over the local dialect. One hand stretched toward the timbered ceiling, palm up, as if to say 'beautifully constructed, yes?' The other hand wished to place its thumb within his leather belt, as if to answer, 'I'm above such things, please do not bother me." But that hand had trouble finding the belt, and it became entangled within the folds of his cloak.

The conversation within the room dulled to a minor hum.

Fergus ached to help, but not knowing what to do, he decided it was better to show a brave face, and act as if all was normal.

McDougal managed to pass the first table without incident, but only because a quick-witted patron moved his chair to make more room.

The second table was the empty one, and as he passed, his knee leapt sideways. Perhaps, he did this to shake his cloak open so that his thumb could get free and find a roost upon his belt. That is partly what happened; the cloak spread, but the knee smashed one chair into another.

All conversation stopped.

The next table looked to be a group of unshaved soldiers, and the space between tables was most narrow here. It seemed, only a miracle could bring McDougal safely through the gap.

Now, that bumbling hand had finally freed itself. It flew wide with the cloak, soaring out from its folds.

Then, before the cloak could close in upon his body again, the hand dove in fast to finally find its resting place. This happened just as McDougal attempted the passing of the table.

But his hand missed its intended perch and struck the pommel of his sword instead. The sword pivoted at the belt, and as the pommel was forced down, the blade, covered in a leather scabbard, flew upwards. Unfortunately, at the same moment, McDougal turned sideways to pass through the narrow gap between tables. The sword accelerated, arcing.

It happened in an instant. One condescending and scowling face, sat in the sword's whistling path.

There was a loud, sickening slap, as the flat of the blade sent the man sprawling back amongst his companions. They at once heaved him to his feet and back towards McDougal. The man spun round, with eyes rolling even as he reached for his weapon. The smell of drink was heavy upon his person as he fell to the floor, and didn't move.

For a few moments nobody else moved either. One of the soldiers said something, but all Fergus heard was a name—Aramis. McDougal's hood had fallen back, and he was staring, mouth open, at the unconscious man. Then Fergus looked also, he was older now, and with a close-cropped beard, but it was indeed Aramis, and he felt fear as he looked upon that face.

One of the soldiers snarled. He was young, with sunken eyes, and high cheek bones. He had a mean looking countenance; but it was partly put on, he tried overly hard to make out that he was tough. He was known as Rush. "You've laid out our Captain."

McDougal seemed to shake himself back to the present. But what came out of his mouth hadn't occurred since they were boys. It left when their childhood torturer, Aramis, had been driven away, and now it was back. "I d-d-d .... I d-d-d- ...I d-didn't mean to."

The stutter frightened Fergus more than battles, dragons, or bog-land. Rush began to push his way around the table, drawing a double edged dirk from a leg scabbard. He withdrew the weapon, slow and deliberate, as he spoke, "It's only right that we lay you down by his side. I'll give you a few seconds to lay down on your own." At this, Aramis' men laughed, though weakly. Fergus guessed by their demeanor—they had never seen their captain insensible—and they were unsure of what to do.

"It was an a-a- accident," McDougal stuttered. His shoulders slumped under his cloak. He made no move to defend himself; instead he looked intently upon Aramis' face.

Rush saw the easy victory, and took a moment to note the spectators. He held their gaze, and smirked. Rush rolled his shoulders, flexing muscles. He swaggered, and then stopped short.

Fergus was moving towards him—his long hickory spear tapping the floor with each step—and leisurely, he closed the gap. He timed their meeting as Rush reached to move the last chair between them.

Rush left his hand upon the chair, uncertain now. He was supposed to have the advantage, yet Fergus was coming at him, intense, confident. Fergus stared into the young face.

"Accidents do happen," Fergus said, calmly. "Like the way you just spoke with my lord, I'm sure that was an accident. But you're not saying you're sorry, in fact you're not saying anything. Sheath your knife and we'll just let it go."

Fergus laid his hardened hand upon Rush's and held it there. Rush tried to pull away. Fergus raised an eyebrow and shook his head. Unnerved, Rush made to strike with his knife. Like a snake bite, the hickory spear struck out, and cracked Rush upon the wrist. The knife clattered to the floor.

"You see that, another accident, a person could get hurt around here. Badly hurt. Why don't you sit down before that happens? I'll just kick that knife out of the way so nobody trips on it."

Rush didn't move, so Fergus shoved the chair hard, into his knees, and spun his falling body onto the seat. Rush ceased to resist, rubbing his knees with his one good hand, the other wrist lay limp against his chest.

There were four men left at the table, and they broke from their stupor and began to rise.

"No, No, No, that's quite all right, fellows," Fergus said. "Don't get up on our account, I insist." This last he said deliberately, as he swung his heavy spear in a half-circle, the thick metal point poised over the unconscious face of Aramis. He tightened his grip upon Rush's shoulder. Rush grimaced. The soldiers settled back down, grumbling.

"Very good." Fergus lifted his gaze to the bar, where stood two of the filthiest men he'd ever seen. One of them held a steaming plate of food in each arm, forgotten, as they watched. Fergus was unsure who to address, but thought it best to keep the momentum moving in his favor. "Inn Keeper, we'll have a room now. Just point us in the right direction."

The man with the food, who they would later understand to be Flemup, looked past Fergus towards the snake plumed guardian at the door. Flemup gulped. "We haven't any more rooms ... sir."

Then thinking of the giant Oded and the grizzly, he said, "We'll sleep in the stables then, and we'll take that food for our dinner."

Fergus, who had been trained as a ranger, had a special gift for imitating sounds of the forest, and he could whistle sweet melodies that sounded as if the angels themselves were playing their heavenly instruments. He began the well known tune, 'Gabriana,' and kept the hall mesmerized as he and McDougal wound their way to Flemup. Tossing a silver piece upon the bar, they took the plates, and Fergus held the indicated door for his lord.

Before following him into the night, Fergus caught the eyes of Rush. He saw hate staring back.

As they walked into the unlit courtyard, they paused to let their eyes adjust.

McDougal spoke. He sounded tired. "Whether to-night still, or tomorrow, we'll have them to deal with."

Blood Pudding

The smells and sounds of the stable made it easy to find. The stable ran a hundred and fifty feet along the north palisade, thirty feet deep. It was an immense structure made mostly from stone, matching the Inn. Forty or so horses were corralled outside. Soft light came from a corner within.

"It is you who should be Lord Fergus, and I not even worthy to be your man," McDougal said. The faithful, hopeful, and enduring spirit of McDougal was flickering.

They stood in the shadows of the stable, just inside the moon-line drawn across the ground, still and silent. Awkwardly, Fergus laid a hand on McDougal's shoulder, as he had seen McDougal do so many times to himself and others.

"Sir. When we were fourteen, do you remember when your father made me your shield-bearer?"

"Yes."

"Just before, he brought me to Theodoro's Pass."

McDougal suddenly lifted his head. "Yes? Did he speak of Theodoro?"

"No, he spoke of you."

McDougal said nothing, but his shoulders quavered—leaned—eager.

"He said you were different from the rest of the family. He said God had given you two special gifts which were stronger in you than he had ever seen in anyone else."

"Truly?" McDougal said, his voice quavering.

"Truly. He said the first gift was a physical agility and dexterity that had surpassed grown men since you were eleven. Your natural ability from God: physical prowess, superior concentration, grasp of the situation, faith in the one who guides your arm, and your skills acquired truly made you the greatest of warriors. Remember, Sir, you were only fourteen when he spoke of you this way."

It was too dark to be sure, but knowing McDougal as he did, and the slight change in his stature, Fergus could see the tears without really seeing them.

"The second gift, he said, was more important and valuable than the first. All men must fight against pride. He said men with half your skill usually fall prey to its control. So God gave you an awkwardness of form and speech to protect you from the pride which otherwise you surely would have succumbed. Your father grabbed me by the arms and said, 'Mind me, Fergus. It is a gift from God.'

"Then he spoke of the character he and your mother had worked hard to instill in you, and that it was the second gift which would help cement them in your breast, to become a godly man. For to this man will God look, even to him that is poor and of a contrite spirit, and trembles at his word."

"But why," McDougal asked, "have you not told me this before? Fifteen years."

"I thought, I could help ..." Now it was Fergus who looked down.

"Improve me?" McDougal asked.

"Yes. Your father said it was a gift, and I tried to rid you of it."

"Well, I am glad you've told me. You are the most faithful friend a man could have. Your words have hurt some, but they have healed more. Faithful are the wounds of a friend. Now, I will trust my father, and I hope you shall too, and perhaps not be too ashamed of me ..."

"No, sir, I am your man. It is me who I am ashamed of."

McDougal trembled with joy. He grasped Fergus in his arms and squeezed enthusiastically.

"Even if I shall stutter in the face of my enemies," McDougal said, "I will know that I am blessed by the Creator, and I shall be content."

"Yes, sir, I beg you, sir, please put me down, sir." Fergus barely held on to their dinner, as one plate seemed especially ready to fall.

"That's right, Fergus; you are one who likes his formalities." McDougal's white grinning teeth shone despite the dark. "What do you say, let's eat our supper, find the boy and deliver our warning. Perhaps we can collect Gimcrack and be gone before —"

They both heard it. It was a whisper that sounded like Gimcrack's name being repeated. Faint as distant thunder on a clear day, they doubted what they had heard.

"Gimcrack ..." McDougal called softly on the cool night air. Nothing.

Again McDougal whispered, but this time it was Thiery's name.

There was a quick intake of breath, of surprise. Seconds later the wall moved slightly, giving Fergus an off balance feeling, like the earth might be swaying beneath his feet. His mind quickly righted itself when he realized it was a door—unnoticed before—that was silently opening at their side.

Strong animal odors wafted forth, and a little voice said. "Who are you?"

Then almost immediately there was another voice from beyond the door, puzzling; because it boomed deeply even as it whispered; it commanded as an adult even as the words sounded as if they were formed by a child. It said, "Don't move or we'll, we'll ... what will we do Suzie? ..."

"We want to ask them some questions," Suzie's little voice prompted.

"Don't move or we'll ask you some questions," the deep voice said. Suzie giggled.

"We won't move," McDougal said with a gallant bow. "Ask away, sweet lady and sir protector."

"I do protect her. You shouldn't tell me what to do, I don't even know you," The deep voice responded, which they now saw was Oded the Bear, as the door had opened further and a faint glow outlined his massive form.

"Yes, I see." McDougal was taken aback in mid bow. "I meant only to say, Sir Protector, as your title."

"I don't have a title to protect."

"Ah, well, I meant only to compliment you, sir."

"Ohhhhh," Oded drew out the word, and they could see him lean down towards Suzie and whisper, though it was not so quiet that they could not hear. "First he tried to be bossy, and when that didn't work, then he tried to flatter me. Maybe we should close the door. A man that flattereth his neighbor spreadeth a net for his feet—"

McDougal interrupted, "No, Oded, all I meant was that we saw you in the woods today and—"

Oded's hand sprung up to block his view of McDougal's face. He began a quiet conversation with the little girl.

"They were spying on us, and they know my name, and I didn't tell them. Oh boy. Suzie, I think I better close the door. Remember what Count Rosencross said."

"Yes, Oded, but I think they might be good, and we haven't any friends. I liked their story very much and maybe we've misjudged them. If they are good, then it would be nice to have some friends who could help us."

"How can we know for sure? The Count said someone might try to hurt you. I'm supposed to keep you safe. Look how those two skulk in the dark like thieves."

Fergus stood a little straighter and eyed his lord, but McDougal just looked through the doorway smiling.

"I have an idea," Suzie said, clapping her hands. "When I look at your face I can tell you are nice, and when I look at some people I can be pretty sure they aren't. Maybe we should shine a light on their faces."

"Okay, let's try it."

Suzie disappeared from the gap in the door, and a moment later returned with a lamp. She proceeded to ask their names, profession, and what their favorite dessert was. McDougal's boyish grin won them over immediately.

"Oh, I think his face is very honest and kind. And don't you think it unusual for a lord to look so friendly. They have so many reasons to be proud. What do you think, Oded?"

"I guess lords can't help being bossy."

"Yes, and he only told you to do a very noble thing. To protect me. lords should have the protection of ladies and children first on their minds, and so I think we shall like him and trust him further."

"Okay." Oded's eyes which had been narrow, suddenly ballooned open and a lopsided grin spread across his face, filling his cheeks with dimples. He put out his hand to McDougal and shook it heartily. "Welcome to our stables. Want to see my bear?"

Suzie tugged on the corner of his leather jerkin. "We forgot about the other one."

Oded narrowed his eyes to slits again and looked upon Fergus.

Fergus could not bring himself to smile for them. The whole pretense seemed beneath him and the idea of being accepted or not because of one's countenance irked his sense of logic. They would have to see by his carriage and manner, that skulking in shadows with evil intentions was something he just did not do.

"He's awfully serious," Oded said.

It felt like minutes went by, though perhaps it was only seconds. Fergus realized with a pang that their scrutiny was becoming difficult to bear. But bear it he would. His brow felt warm.

Suzie turned to McDougal. "Does he smile much?"

"Not much, but when he does, it's all the better for the lack of its appearing. Why don't you smile for them, Fergus?"

Smiling on command was so foreign and shocking to Fergus, that for a second, he lost his composure completely; an embarrassed scowl appeared before his stony face could be mustered back. Suzie gasped.

"Really, Fergus," McDougal admonished. "That will not do." Then turning to Oded and Suzie he said, "It's not like him to joke, I'm not sure what came over him."

Maybe they would suddenly be attacked by Aramis and his soldiers—that would be better than this interrogation. McDougal was raising his eyebrows higher and higher. A trickle of sweat rolled down Fergus' forehead.

"Alright, sir, it's just that, well this is quite unconventional. I find it odd, sir, that I must prove my character with my smile."

"Great fun, isn't it?" McDougal said enthusiastically.

"I see, sir." Fergus looked into the lamp light, gritted his teeth, and widened his mouth, lifting his cheek muscles so that the edges of his lips would curve up and not down.

"Oh dear," Suzie whispered.

"Is he trying to scare her?" Oded asked. "He looks like he's trying to scare her."

Fergus aborted the attempt immediately. He looked at McDougal, his eyes pleading. "Please, sir, I find this rather difficult, perhaps another test would be better suited for me."

Suzie recovered upon seeing how discomfited Fergus was. "How about your favorite dessert, I love to make dessert!"

Fergus was an honest man, and though he had misgivings about his answer, he stood straight, stared into the lamp again, and said. "Blood pudding. I do enjoy blood pudding."

His three interrogators stared blankly at him. McDougal raised his hand, partly covering his eyes and forehead. Then, slowly, he shook his head back and forth.

Oded's deep rumble of a voice and Suzie's sweet cadence harmonized. "eeeccccwwwwww!" Even their shoulders raised and shuddered in similar fashion.

The Guardians

Fergus could see that with every question and with every test they invented, his true and faithful heart was misinterpreted. Not to mention, most of their examination made no sense. McDougal seemed to be enjoying himself immensely, because in many ways, he looked at life, and even approached his God, through the wondering eyes of a child. This at least, Fergus could take some pleasure in, for it was not yet an hour earlier that his lord had been suffering.

But it was taking its toll. Fergus was a very serious minded adult. Everything had its fitting and acceptable way. This interrogation certainly did not fit into the proper way of things. A little girl who was a child, the son of a giant with the mind of a child, and his very own lord in the spirit of a child, were unsettling Fergus with illogical and bothering blows of innocence.

It was McDougal who finally came to his rescue by giving one of his thoroughly rousing speeches. He spoke of their boyhood adventures, of Fergus's love of God, and all that is loyal, dutiful, and good. Suzie's eyes were wide. With every description she would grasp her hands together and with quick intakes of breath say things like 'oh,' and 'wow,' and 'oh my'—she gazed admiringly back and forth from Fergus to McDougal.

"And so," McDougal said with a flourish of his arms, "I introduce into our new band of friends, my most faithful and true friend, Fergus Leatherhead."

Suzie's characteristic clapping caused Fergus to smile in spite of himself, and this smile was a real one. Suzie flung herself around his legs. "Welcome, welcome, Sir Fergus. Oh, this is wonderful, don't you think so, Oded?"

But Oded had a strange look upon his face.

"I believe he's holding his breath," McDougal said.

"Oh dear," Suzie said, staring. "He must have the hiccups." Oded shook his head back and forth. He was beginning to look a little blue. "Or he's trying not to laugh." Oded shook his head up and down.

He began to totter, when he finally inhaled deeply, grasping the door jamb for support. Recovering, he reached his hand out, and shook Fergus's enthusiastically. "Welcome, friend Fergus." He spoke it in his slow way, but there was a sparkle in his eye, and it was evident that he was trying not to smile.

The rest of the party was smiling now, watching Oded's antics. "What's so funny, Oded?" Suzie asked.

"I don't want to be rude."

"Please tell us; just tell us in a polite way."

"Okay, let me think." Oded set his giant hammer down, cupped his chin within his hands, and softly patted both cheeks with his fingers. The minutes began to drag on.

"Do you mind very much if we come in and eat our dinner while you think?" McDougal asked.

And so they entered the stable, walking its length toward the far end, where a sort of cottage room waited. They passed horses, a pack of hounds, and Oded's grizzly, whose name was Griz. It was an impressive beast.

Suzie said hello to the animals by name as they passed. Oded thrummed upon his cheek with one hand, and swung his war hammer-chest in the other, occasionally whispering to himself.

The room was furnished with a large table and chairs, a bunk bed, and a stone fireplace. Everything was clean and neat. The room's competing decorations were weapons and flowers. Pole-arms, swords, and bows hung upon walls and from the rafters, and placed near each one was a bouquet of fresh or dried flowers. Bunched herbs hung drying from the ceiling.

They set their food upon the table and waited for their host to seat himself. Fergus looked at his plate, for the first time realizing just how hungry he was. The food was cold now but it looked surprisingly good.

"I got it," Oded said. "My first clue. Is everyone ready? I hope it's not too hard. Okay, here I go. It rhymes with game and it starts with the letter N."

Suzie giggled. "Name?"

"That was fast, I should have known you would get it. Okay let me think of the next clue."

"Perhaps you'd think better while sitting down," McDougal said, looking at his food.

"Why would that make me think better?"

"Hmmm, well, Fergus, any ideas why that might help Oded to think better?"

"Perhaps thoughts don't have to work so hard if your head is closer to the ground," Fergus said.

"Do you think so?" Oded asked.

"No, not really, but I suppose it could be possible. I sometimes have trouble sleeping because my mind seems to work very hard when I lay down."

"Brilliant deduction," McDougal said. "Why don't you take a seat Oded?"

"I had better lay down, so I can get an extra good clue." Oded threw himself down on a pile of straw in the corner.

"Some food might help us figure out his clue, sir," Fergus offered. "We could share our meals and have a dinner party."

"Excellent idea! feed the brain and all that."

"A dinner party!" Suzie trembled all over, finally giving vent by bouncing. "Would that be okay, Oded? We have some bread and cheese in the pantry, and I could start a kettle warming."

"Okay, you start without me. I gotta think."

Dividing the food into four portions, they prayed their thanksgivings to God, and ate.

"Truly," McDougal said, "taste and see that the Lord is good. Never before have I said so with such ardor."

Suzie blushed as they ate, grinned, and grinned some more.

"And this bread, this is the best bread I've ever tasted. Whoever the cook of this Inn is, they'll never let her go."

"Oh but they will," Suzie said. "Count Rosencross is master here, and he's told Oded to take me away very soon, before the Dragon Priests get me."

"Do you mean to say that you're responsible for this delicious fare we've been partaking of?"

Suzie clapped her hands again. "Well, I made the bread, and I made up the recipe for the meal they served you."

"You are a treasure, more valuable than rubies. Now what is this about Dragon Priests?"

"Okay everybody, are you ready?" Oded, raised himself to his knees. "I think it worked. This is the second part of the name. It rhymes with bed and sits on top of your shoulders. Try to figure it out while I think of a clue for the first part of the name." Oded laid back down upon the straw.

"The Count has been very nice to me," Suzie said. "And he likes my cooking too, and he likes for me to sing him songs sometimes. Yesterday, he came and told us that he must give me up, that the Dragon Priests didn't like people who called on the God of Noah, and that they might do me harm."

"Yes," Oded said. "And he dismissed her uncle from being uncle any more. And he said that I would be like her new uncle, and that I would be her ... what's that word Suzie? The one I always forget."

"Guardian."

"Yes, that's it, her guardian. And so I have a very big guardian responsibility. He left for Hradcanny today and said I should take her away from here before long."

"But how can one dismiss an uncle?" McDougal asked. "Was he an unsuitable and dishonest fellow then?"

And so Suzie told the story of Elvodug, who was not truly her uncle. She sadly admitted that they showed no signs of love or care for anything but riches. They used to set her upon a corner to beg, and how they would send her into small passages under the earth to rob graves, and explore caverns into which they could not fit.

Through one such expedition, she found a sack of gold. For two years they lived well. Flemup and Elvodug hired a nursemaid to care for Suzie while they caroused in the city. She was a godly woman who took seriously the admonition to teach children of God's ways, when they rise up, when they walk in the way, and when they lie down. And Suzie learned to love the Lord.

When the gold was gone, they hired on with Count Rosencross, and that is where they had been the last six months. Her nurse had died. Then, one night she heard them speaking in their sleep, as they often did. It was an argument.

Flemup said that it was he that found Suzie, and therefore he should get a bigger share in whatever riches she brought in. Elvodug said that it had been his idea to keep her, and to assume the role of uncle: what a grand stroke of genius that had been, and therefore he deserved the greater share of wealth.

Then Suzie had met and befriended Thiery. He had adopted her as his sister, and then he had caught some dangerous sickness, and the priests had quarantined him in a tent. He died the next day.

So, their warning had been too late, for Fergus remembered that tent, and the apple peel, and the dead insects which had eaten from it. He wondered at it, but kept his musings to himself.

"What scoundrels, rogues, scalawags," McDougal's voice rose higher and higher. "You poor sweet child. So young, and so much hardship. If you'll take me, and Oded is in agreement, I offer myself, as a fellow guardian, to keep you safe from physical and spiritual danger." He had gotten to his knees before Suzie, and was holding her hands.

"Is that okay, Oded?" Suzie asked softly, her eyes brimmed with tears—smiling eyes.

"Okay."

"Splendid. Then we shall be your true friends, the guardians and watchers for your soul."

Oded stood up now, towering over the room. He picked up McDougal and Suzie, and hugged them. "My new guardian brother and my precious little Suzie." Putting them down he said, "I have the last clue. It's the first part of the word." Pointing to a bouquet of dried heather, he said, "It rhymes with those, only it's something you can wear. This thinking close to the ground thing is really smart."

"Okay." Suzie posed as if deep in thought. "You said we are trying to figure out a name. The name has two parts. The second part rhymes with bed and sits upon someone's shoulders. That would be 'head'. The first part of the name is something you wear and rhymes with heather ..." Suzie's eyes suddenly went wide, and now she too tried not to smile.

"Remember, when you figure it out, don't laugh too hard." Oded looked at Suzie and McDougal, and leaned his head meaningfully towards Fergus. He whispered with his deep booming voice, "Some people might feel bad if they knew how funny their name was."

Fergus pretended he didn't hear, and took another bite of bread.

Bad Guys

Fergus opened his eyes with a start. Wings flapped about the barn, and swooped down over his face. "Morning. Morning. Morning," the bird called as it circled three times and then perched upon Oded's chest.

"Good Morning, Birdie," Oded said. "How's the weather, Birdie? Weather, Birdie?"

Birdie flew to a shuttered window, and landing on its uppermost edge, pushed its beak against the wall. The shutter swung wide and Birdie hopped down to the ledge, peering into the morning sky.

"Pretty day," Birdie said.

"Thank you." Oded stood up and pointed at the open doorway leading into the barn area. Birdie landed upon his finger. "Bad guys?" Oded whispered.

The little bird flew into the barn. A moment later it returned to Oded's shoulder and more quietly this time, said "All clear."

"I say," McDougal said. "That's quite remarkable. Will that bird be joining our party?" For before turning in, they had all agreed it would be best to leave on the morrow. The Count had given Oded leave to do whatever necessary to keep Suzie safe—and then earlier in the previous day he had stopped by and told them to make preparations to disappear, to be gone before the week was out.

They had decided that Suzie would work the morning shift in the kitchen, so as not to draw attention to anything unusual, and then she and Oded would take their normal jaunt into the surrounding hills—only they wouldn't be coming back. McDougal, Fergus, and Gimcrack were to join them on the road to Hradcanny, an hour later.

Oded kissed the bird's beak. "Yes. I love Birdie, and she's smart. I have to leave the hounds behind, because they aren't mine. I'll miss them. But Birdie and Griz, and the two biggest stallions are mine."

Fergus saw that a lamp was burning low—everyone had been awake and at the table but him. He felt the shame of it as he donned his sword belt, and sat with the others. Suzie laid a plate of bread and cheese before him. At least his master had not had to serve himself breakfast.

"I better not be late, Oded," Suzie said gently.

"Okay, I'll walk you over."

"And I'll join you, and bring some breakfast to Gimcrack," McDougal said, getting to his feet. Fergus pushed his untouched plate from him and made to rise, but McDougal pressed upon his shoulder. "Oh no, Fergus, you break your fast, and choose us three horses when you're through. Oded tells me that the horses corralled outside, closest to the barn, are for sale. When you've chosen, you can put them in one of the empty stalls. We do have the funds for it?"

"We do, sir. But I could eat later, and join you." Fergus disliked contradicting his master, but it seemed worse to leave his master's side when danger threatened. He was sure there was more to Witch Esla's prophecy than a mere guess at the future—somebody wanted McDougal dead. And now, after all this time, Aramis was here, and he'd awaken to an angry ache in his head.

"No, you eat. Find me a horse tall enough that I'll not look the fool upon it."

"Very good, sir."

And so they walked the length of the barn. Fergus could not help but turn and watch them go. Suzie looked back. She waved. He waved in return, and then the door swung shut.

Working with horses, his weapons would only be in the way, but if McDougal needed his shield-bearer, they must be close. So thinking, he hung his sword, and leaned his hickory spear against the door jamb. The spear was thicker than most, but with perfect balance, and incredible strength; he ran his fingers along the smooth surface. If while he worked the horses, there was trouble, the door would be close. If in the stalls, he must still come that way to help his master.

Fergus passed the hounds, their eyes followed him, but they didn't bother to lift their heads. Griz slept. The horses were quiet.

Returning to his plate, he poured himself a drink and sat down to eat. Halfway through his meal, the little bird landed on his shoulder. Fergus had to admit—Oded was a superior beast-master. He wondered how good a ranger he could be with all that bulk traversing the forest. Then he remembered when Griz and Oded had emerged from the woods the previous day. Neither had made a sound.

"That was a smart trick, Birdie. Will you do it for me?" Fergus held out his hand and pointed back into the stables.

The bird alighted on his finger. Fergus smiled.

Fergus imitated Oded and whispered the command, "Bad guys?"

Once again, Birdie flew about the barn, into the loft, behind the hay bales, into the shadows, and then returned to Fergus's shoulder. If you had any idea of an enemy lurking there, it was easy to see the advantage they would have. Piles of hay to hide behind, a loft, and animals which would not raise an alarm at an intruder—for the comings and goings of warriors would be commonplace.

Enough light streamed through a few windows to soften the dark, but many things were still in shadow. Dust swirled through the streaks of light wherever the bird had passed.

Fergus's smile disappeared at Birdie's quiet response, "Bad guys!"

He had been so concerned for McDougal, that he had overlooked his own safety. His weapons were fifty feet away, excepting his knife. But was there truly someone there, or was the bird mistaken? He hadn't heard the door open, or had he, and then dismissed it as any one of a number of sounds at the Hilltop Inn.

Trying to look natural, Fergus took another bite of cheese and looked upon the walls and into the rafters for the closest weapon, and one he might be most proficient with. Glancing occasionally into the barn, there was one spot in particular that caused Fergus some worry, for two of the hounds were looking in that direction.

Before he had made up his mind just what to do, that shadowy place came to life and stepped into a patch of sun.

It was Rush. He was only thirty feet away, holding a double shot crossbow, and smiling, evil like.

"Come for some breakfast?" Fergus pushed a chair out some.

"You made a fool of me." Rush leveled the crossbow at Fergus's chest.

"Perhaps. Are you seeking an apology?"

Rush was enjoying himself. It was evident what he wanted; there was hate in his eyes. "I think you know what I've come for."

Fergus could flip the table, and perhaps escape the first bolt, but he didn't think his chances were good. Rush looked quick, and ready. And there'd be a second bolt.

Then he got to thinking, just maybe that bird had been taught other things too. His mind was racing, it might work. Fergus slowly raised his arm and pointed at the double crossbow. "That's a pretty piece there."

Birdie hopped onto his fingers.

"I don't miss, and it'll pass clear through a man at this range." It was evident that he wanted to see Fergus frightened before he'd pull the trigger. Fergus was afraid, but he'd not show it. He bunched his muscles, ready to spring, as he called out softly.

"Birdie, attack!"

And that's just what that bird did. Oded was indeed a first rate beast-master. A man can't have something fly at his face without reacting, even a small bird. Rush ducked and threw up his free hand to protect himself. He also fired.

The wind from it whistled past Fergus's ear as he stepped onto the chair, the table, and then jumped and pulled himself into the rafters above. The only thing close by was a wooden timber-framing mallet used to drive timbers and pegs together during the construction of the barn. The head on it was close to a foot wide and almost as tall. Someone had left it gathering dust on a support girder directly above the table.

Grabbing it up, Fergus sprang across the trusses, towards Rush; only he was twelve feet above him. The beams were four feet apart, and it was dark, but they were massive beams, almost a foot wide, so Fergus ran quickly—knowing he couldn't let Rush get his bearings or he'd be easy enough to shoot down. It was a gamble, but nothing else had come to mind.

One step sent a sharp pain up his leg as he hit the girder smack in the middle of his foot. But momentum carried him forward. He heard the flapping of Birdie, and then Rush was directly below him.

Reaching down and swinging the mallet as he held the rafter with his free hand, Fergus strained every muscle to keep his perch and strike. Rush raised the crossbow. Not to shoot, but to block the blow. He was too late.

The mallet knocked him from his feet, and the crossbow clattered to the floor. There was a soft groan from Rush, and then he just lay there, crumpled in a heap upon the ground. Fergus dropped to the floor and felt for his pulse. It was a mean blow, but he was still breathing. He was tough; Fergus would give him that.

A follower of the God of Noah could defend himself, and fight for family, friends, country, and those who needed defending, but he could not kill an unarmed enemy. In fact, Fergus felt he must help this man who had sought to kill him. He shuddered as he recalled the sound of that wallop. Rush's face was swelling, turning an ugly blue and black, his head lay limp, perhaps unnaturally so.

Buckling his sword back on, Fergus lifted Rush into his arms, and carried him across the courtyard, into the Inn, and laid him upon the bar. Some of his mercenary friends jumped up from a table.

Fergus turned sharply towards them. "He's had an accident. If he lives, tell him not to come hunting me again." Aramis wasn't there. Maybe he hadn't recovered from the night before. But this time his men acted with some readiness. Two of them sauntered close to the door.

Just as if he meant to all along, Fergus sidestepped the bar and walked into the kitchen. He had no need for another fight, especially being outnumbered, and without his hickory spear. Taking the lay of the land was a constant, almost unconscious practice for a ranger. The wilderness was alive with dangers for an unsuspecting man, and it wasn't always the creatures that came hunting. You had to pay attention to high ground, possible places of ambush, ways of escape, alternate routes, and if you had an animal with you, whether a horse or hound or something more unusual like that Birdie, you better learn quick to know their signs of unease, for they could know a thing well before a man.

So Fergus knew there was a back entrance to the kitchen, where he'd seen the cooks throwing their scraps in a heap. From there, it was only fifty feet to the stables. He didn't know if they'd give chase, or wait for another opportunity now that he'd slipped from their immediate grasp, but it was best to be ready. Without Aramis or Rush pushing them into it, he figured they'd let it lie, for now anyway.

A woman was cutting potatoes, and Elvodug was alone in a corner, armed with a cleaver. He looked like a sly one, nobody to turn your back on. Suzie wasn't there. There was no time to enquire if he wanted a safe retreat through the back door. But he had an uneasy feeling, and later, looking back, Fergus thought that Elvodug had suddenly turned pale under his grease and grime stained face.

After an hour, the horses were saddled, and all their gear was ready, including some food, when Oded burst into the stables. McDougal followed right behind.

"Give chase, get them, we've got to get them," Oded groaned.

"Get who?" Fergus asked.

Oded didn't answer, but he ran to a cupboard, slung a pack over his shoulder, and opened Griz's stable.

"Sir, what's happening?"

McDougal led his horse from the barn as he spoke. "It seems some Dragon Priests came and took Suzie away, took her upon horseback towards Hradcanny."

"How do you know this?"

"Oded went to bring her home, and Elvodug and Flemup, they just poured forth the story as soon as they saw Oded's grim face. I think those two thought they'd seen their last day as he picked them up and swung them upside down. Anyone who thinks Oded's just a simpleton better watch out."

Oded growled a command to the gate-keeper. The gate swung open, and Griz and Oded disappeared into the forest, while McDougal and Fergus mounted their horses and rode along the highway for Hradcanny.

"Where's Oded going?"

"He said that he wanted to get his brother's help, something about not taking any chances with another child under his protection, so we're to meet him at the Tavern of the Seven Talons. A place just a few miles outside Hradcanny's eastern wall, joined between the Nonnus of Bacchus and the Nonna of Urania, Queen of Heaven. And we're to look for trail-sign in case the priests leave the road."

"What about Gimcrack?"

McDougal's features were tense. "We followed his tracks to the highway, but we couldn't tell where he went from there. It seems I was wrong. He left us."

Dragon Tracks

The lingering effects of the poison had worn off at last—for that is what Thiery now believed had happened. He had come to terms with the idea that his own father had tried to kill him, a sacrifice to false gods.

He thought of the morning, only a few days ago, when his priestly father had come by the tent, to say good bye to his dead son. It seemed that maybe he had been remorseful, or at least ... saddened. There were others who sacrificed their children to the gods, not because they wanted to, but because they believed they must. Deceived by a false belief.

Thiery had always dreamed of one day finding his father, but now what? Well, he had an adopted sister, and he loved Oded. They at least could be his family. So he must let them know he still lived, and see if they would come away with him. If not, he would be alone, for a time anyway, for he could not stay in the employ of Count Rosencross. All those Dragon Priests would surely attempt another sacrifice.

In God he would trust. Yes, he would seek the Creator, and seek the betterment of others, and in so doing he would be at peace in this world, even if he had no family. Still, he could not quite let his father go, perhaps he would repent of what he had done … Thiery didn't even know his father's name.

He must forgive him. He must pray.

It was early morning, before the sun had risen. Today they would leave.

"I also have a good friend in you Horatio." The wolf had sensed Thiery's melancholy and had leaned his three hundred pounds against the boy. Just in the two weeks it took to befriend him, and begin training, Thiery could see the muscles and weight swell almost daily upon Horatio. He'd be an important part of keeping Thiery alive, and from being afraid.

"We've got something to do before we leave. If I truly hit that dragon in the eye, there's a chance, God willing, that he's gone off to die. With God's help, I'd likely be the youngest ranger to slay a dragon."

Great hunters, rangers, and especially dragon slayers were well respected. There was a place for them at most anyone's hearth, and even outlaws treated them with respect. To hang a large dragon claw or tooth from your belt could go a long way in keeping an arrow or sword out of your belly, and it could open doors, even a king's door.

Horatio leapt about at Thiery's excited tone. "There'll be none of that on the trail; we'll be like the mouse today. Got it?"

Horatio paused, eyes intent upon Thiery's. That was good. Thiery gave him a command and Horatio crawled; another command and Horatio leapt through the air snarling; yet another and Horatio ran away only to circle back behind a supposed enemy, alert, and ready.

"Good boy." They had covered much in the last three days, and he was anxious to show Oded their progress.

Thiery buried the fallen soldier's weapons and armor within the sandy soil of the lower cave, and left just as it was getting light. Some of the gold hung in his pouch, and a few pieces he had sewed into his clothing.

Thiery had learned to read sign, and track well, but this dragon would take no skill to follow. Some of its tracks made inch deep impressions, and they were almost two feet long. Cautiously they followed them for about a mile. The creature was hurt badly, for its trail told a tale of staggering, sometimes falling, and other times running headlong into trees or rocky outcrops.

The forest gave way to a clearing of boulders and clumps of grass. Directly ahead was a hillside, seemingly cut in two, its crest jutted forward to create an overhanging cliff, beneath which the rocks gaped, forming a large but shallow cavern that bent to the left and out of sight—its furthest recesses dark.

There she was, about twenty five feet from head to tail, sprawled upon the ground, an arrow deeply embedded, protruding from her eye. This was the night terror which had almost caught him in the storm.

She made no move now.

Horatio and Thiery froze at the edge of the wood, ready to run at the slightest stir. Thiery's heart was pounding loud. Horatio's ears were pricked forward.

It was no wonder that Igi Forkbeard's men had been so brutally slain, and so quickly. Thiery thought on the power of God to create such things, and he was overcome with awe—he felt small—who was he that God should be mindful of him?

The danger felt like something tangible in the air. He didn't like it, but after twenty minutes, and still no movement, Thiery tossed a rock at her—if she were alive that should have done something.

Inching forward, he stepped upon a dry stick. The snap sent his heart pounding again, and he realized the sounds of the forest were different here, hushed. Was it because the dragon had kept much away by its presence alone, or was there something more?

Drawing closer, Thiery had to cover his nose with his tunic, for the air was foul. It certainly smelled dead. One of its back legs stretched upon a rock. Taking his newly acquired short-sword, Thiery hacked once, and stopped to listen. Then quickly, two more blows—he had severed three, five inch long claws.

Shoving them into his belt-pouch, he suddenly noticed other tracks, much smaller than the dragons, but exactly the same kind ... young ones. Judging by their tracks, they might be eight or ten feet tall. There were at least two of them—one imprint showed a toe bent as if it had been broken at one time and not healed right, the other pairs were normal.

Images and memories of the fear that had come upon him flashed through his mind ... The night terror standing in the wood, watching, waiting ... the lightning flash, and the moments of the chase through sheets of rain.

And now Thiery felt as if he couldn't move. He could sense the others were near, but where?

A low growl from Horatio—Thiery's limbs became unstuck, and they were both running back through the forest, back to the cave. It was a wild, hastening sprint through the trees, weaving, ducking under branches, and leaping the underbrush.

Not until they scrambled into the lower cave entrance did they pause to catch their breath, and look behind at their pursuers.

Horatio's hackles were still raised, and Thiery held his sword before him, but only the normal sounds of the forest and the flowing river met them. It was fully light. Thiery laughed at himself, breathing heavily ... perhaps there hadn't really been anything after all.

He was about to learn a lesson he'd not soon forget.

While he'd begun to relax and lower his guard—sword tip touching the sand—Horatio was still fully alert. Oded always told him to keep a watchful eye on your animal, they'll know the thing before you can. That's when it happened.

The screaming attack was so fast and vicious that Thiery had no time to raise his blade. The entrance of the cave was instantly darkened by slashing claws, a gaping mouth with rows of razor sharp teeth, and there was more than one of them ... swift and deadly.

Without thinking he threw himself backwards, rolling into the cavern beyond.

A dragon mouth was so close to his face that he could feel its breath on his cheek. The teeth chomped air inches from him. He kept rolling.

Then his back was to the cave wall and there was no way he could turn and climb without being eaten from behind.

He swung wildly and felt the blade bite. But the dragon's claws brushed his fingers as it clenched upon the weapon. Letting go, he rolled to the side and drew his knife. He had a moment's respite—it was then that Thiery saw just how much trouble they were in.

He had wounded one, but it was still coming at him, though wary this time. And there were not two dragons, but three. Horatio held another at bay; it too was cautious but stalking forward.

The third now had room to maneuver, and he turned towards Thiery. In a few moments it would be all over. He might avoid one, for a time, but two, and as fast as they were, and as winded as he was?

Each breath burned in his chest. His muscles began to shake.

They moved in for the kill.

Wet-fire

People liked to talk of the old ways before the dispersion—that great city of Babel, and the technologies that were carried through the flood from the Old World. But then, the peoples were divided by family groups, given different languages, and scattered upon the face of the earth. Much was lost.

Some family groups were more knowledgeable than others, some more wise, and some who met with more difficulties, dwindled in number so that much of the old world's learning faded or disappeared entirely.

But there were some who thrived. There was talk of a people far to the south who built great towers which reached to the heavens. They were led by Mizraim, grandson of Noah.

King Strongbow was a seeker of the knowledge, and so the peoples round about grew to respect the guilds of alchemy, astrology, engineers, discoverers of witty inventions, herbalists, and other scholars.

Many times while sitting around the fire, Thiery had listened to exciting stories: flying craft that a man could ride within, just like the birds or flying serpents; a powder that when collected in quantity, encapsulated, and ignited, could blow holes in the rocks; and a strange substance remembered as wet-fire that would burn even upon water.

These things and others were discussed by the people, but many of their secrets remained hidden, buried in the graves of their forefathers or whisked away to another land by God's dispersion. Yet some of these secrets were known, but only by a few, and often they were jealously guarded.

One of them came to Thiery's aid now.

Suddenly, the upper cave burst light upon the dim and desperate proceedings below. The dragons paused. They had the advantage of better night vision, but their dilated pupils were facing towards the ledge from which the light poured forth, and they were momentarily blinded.

From the corner of his eye, Thiery could see a man pointing a crossbow-like weapon, with a strange box above the firing mechanism. There was a twang, and then a ball of fire leapt forward, in an instant, a large smear of burning flesh appeared upon the nearest dragon.

The man grabbed a handle and thrust the box forward; while the back of it raised, the front advanced a hook which grabbed the bow-string, then pulling it back into position he fired again. The second dragon's chest burst into flame. Their screams reverberated throughout the cave even as the creatures recoiled and fled into the forest.

Almost as quickly—the chamber's light dimmed.

Thiery didn't move as he let his eyes adjust. He felt Horatio at his side. The entrance to the upper cave slowly became visible and with a command he sent Horatio leaping for it. As he followed, and brushed against the skeleton, he thought he could hear a faint scraping sound, almost like rock grating upon rock or metal.

Thiery fumbled in the half-light, found a lamp and struck the flint, bringing it to life. But the chamber was empty, and the door leading to the ledge surely hadn't opened or it would have been obvious by the sunlight streaming in. Where had the man gone?

He looked into the shadows. The bookcase and bed were back there, but nothing else. Perhaps the bookcase was some kind of door.

He moved it easily enough. There wasn't anything behind.

Why did the man rescue him and then disappear, and how had he gone so quickly? Thiery had never been alone, without friends, for so long, and his young heart ached for one. Especially now that he must make a journey through unknown lands, to contend with beasts and Dragon Priests. And though he had only caught a glimpse of the fellow, there was something about him that seemed familiar.

The bed was a simple mattress, stuffed with grasses, and set upon a rocky ledge. Thiery had slept there each night, and had noticed nothing unusual. His pillow and blankets were shoved up against the far side, and he was sure he hadn't left them that way. Had the mysterious visitor arrived early this morning, tired enough to take a nap? Or …

Thiery pulled upon the bed. It wouldn't move. It seemed strange that the mattress was somehow transfixed to the rock. For ten minutes he searched, when suddenly his fingers felt a stone move, ever so slightly.

He pressed against it. The stone receded further; there was a click, and then the same scraping sound he had heard earlier. The edge of the bed rose, revealing a gaping hole. Stairs, cut into the stone, descended into the dark.

Thiery had not eaten yet this morning, and his hands were still shaking, even his legs felt weak. But for a boy of his disposition, another mountain to climb, or cave to explore was a constant pull upon his adventurous spirit.

And this adventure was prefaced by a secret door. But he had much to consider. He would like to thank the man who had saved him, that seemed only right, and hopefully they could be friends, good friends.

Yet at the same time, Oded and Suzie believed him dead. Now that he was strong again, would it be fair to leave them with that false belief a moment longer than needed? The encounter with the dragons had shaken him, and having a traveling companion, a full grown adult to lean upon seemed wise. But could he find the man, and if he did, would he even want to help?

With these swirling thoughts, and a heavy heart, Thiery kneeled before the bed. He rested his arms upon the upper most step, and with his eyes tightly shut, the words tumbled forth. He spoke to his God for a long while, sometimes in tears, sometimes laughing, always thankful. He prayed mostly for those he knew, and for some whom he barely knew. His voice rose and fell as the minutes passed, and he ended with a time of quiet, almost asleep.

Sometimes a person can feel as if he is being watched. Whether he is alerted to it by a sound, or a glimpse of movement, it is hard to say, but Thiery suddenly had that feeling. Opening his eyes, he found himself looking into the face of a man.

A Friend

Horatio had left the vicinity, laying down near the skeleton, watching for the return of those fearsome dragons in the lower cave. So he had not alerted Thiery to the man who was quietly ascending the stone stairwell.

Thiery gasped and threw himself back. But even as he was scrambling to his feet, recognition startled him even more. "Gimcrack!"

Gimcrack's smile suddenly vanished when a growling wolf sprang around the corner. "Whoa deee doooee!" he blurted, with his hands outstretched.

Thiery reassured Horatio with a calm command. The wolf's fur lay flat again. He sat, watching Gimcrack, his tail wagging.

"Do you need to put a rope on him, or at least your hand? One more leap and I'd not like to think of it."

"It's quite all right, sir, you just startled us is all. He's very good at discerning trouble, and he's already decided you're all right. Though I know he's itching to smell you over, if you don't mind?"

"Oh, umm, I see, yes, I guess that's in order." Gimcrack climbed the rest of the way out of the hidden stairwell, and when Thiery released Horatio with another command, the wolf began his investigation of Gimcrack. Now Gimcrack was a stocky fellow, but at thirteen, Thiery was already much taller, and Horatio's massive wolf head sniffed around the dwarf's neck with all four legs still upon the ground. Gimcrack's agitation was evident, so Thiery called Horatio off.

"Yes, well, very good," Gimcrack said. "I was just about to prepare some breakfast when you wandered into my cave. Would you like to join me?"

"Your cave?"

"Well my cousin Staffsmitten and I claim it together. This here is a lesser gate to Tump Barrows, and Staffsmitten is the honorary gate-keeper." Gimcrack waived his arms about, and thrust his chest forward, raising his voice as if he were giving a great oration to a crowded hall.

Thiery felt the proper respect and wonderment at this disclosure, and showed it plainly on his honest face.

Gimcrack was clearly pleased. "I can see we are going to have an excellent breakfast together, let's hold our wagging tongues till we sit at table, then we can discuss this most miraculous and profitable meeting of ours. For I must say I am more surprised to find you, than you me. And your being here brings to mind many appetizing questions which I shall enjoy more, if I have some food to fill my belly at the same time as my curiosity."

As Gimcrack made the meal, he spoke in a one way conversation, for Thiery was also quite hungry and didn't dare say anything that would slow the breakfast preparations. So, after thanking him heartily for saving them from the dragons, he kept his questions in check.

There was something quite different about this Gimcrack and the one he had warned of the cozen sacrifice almost a week ago.

"Perhaps you are wondering at my great bravery in coming to your aid, and then my disappearance. Well it's a strange story, which fairly begins with you. You see, the presence of those pesty Dragon Priests had begun to make me jumpy. When I heard that they were in the habit of secret sacrifices, I began to imagine all sorts of ways in which they might choose me.

"And then this crazy boy," Gimcrack paused in his work and smiled at Thiery, "set my worst fears just a blazing in my breast. But, it was what you said about the God of Noah and Hell that frazzled my nerves so completely. And then a raspy voiced scary man brought me the very horse you said not to touch and said it was from you."

Thiery's face showed understanding and compassion.

"Yes, and for awhile I wasn't sure if you weren't part of their evil scheme. But I believe differently now. I wouldn't have gotten on the creature either, if it hadn't been for those beating drums in the night, and the Dragon Priests a chanting."

Gimcrack told the whole detailed, and perhaps at times, embellished story of the lyftfloga and swamp; the joining up with Lord McDougal and Fergus Leatherhead; their search for Thiery to warn him that the

Dragon Priests were possibly after him; and their sighting of Oded just last night.

Through it all, Gimcrack stopped to act out much of the story, and so the meal was late indeed. But Thiery had been so enthralled that it wasn't until the food was set before him, that his stomach begged and groaned to be fed. His mouth began to water.

Thiery bowed his head in silent thanksgiving to God, when he was startled by Gimcrack's voice. "Oh God of Noah, I thank you for this food, and for my friend Thiery, and especially for your loving mercy in calling me to you, despite my stubborn heart."

Thiery jumped from his seat, his food momentarily forgotten, and grabbed Gimcrack about his shoulders. "This is too wonderful! Please tell me how it is you've become a follower of God."

"Well, last night after McDougal and Fergus went into that Inn, filled with those accursed priests, I began to think. I thought about my duty to him as my new lord, and I began to worry that there would be trouble, and I felt bad that I hadn't gone with them. So, I wrote them a note, telling them I'd be back by noon the next day, with reinforcements. Only my reinforcement was Staffsmitten, but he wasn't here. He's my best friend and a follower of God also, as you can see by any of his writings that lay about this place. He'll fall over dead when he learns of my conversion.

"Oh, wait, I'm getting ahead of myself. When it got quite dark, and I was nearly to the cave, I began to hear things. I was certain I'd end up eaten by some creature, and I found myself, not calling out to my gods, but to yours. I climbed into the branches of a tree, and asked the God of Noah to keep me safe, and if not, then to let me escape the fires of Hell, and so I rejected all that I had known before and embraced Him. I tied myself into the tree and slept the peaceful sleep of a baby.

"And now, Lord McDougal will be awaiting us within a few hours, and we have just enough time to get there through the passages of Tump Barrows. And while Staffsmitten is not at home, I'll be bringing the very one they sought, and so you see why I'm so amazed at this encounter. Who knows, maybe we'll find another of the Dwarven Brotherhood to help us."

Thiery sat down and began to eat, his heart almost filled to breaking with the joy of Gimcrack's revelation. Struck dumb by it all, he slowly chewed his food, when a sobering thought caused him to turn and looked upon the skeleton.

"Gimcrack, I am overjoyed by what you've done, but I must give you some very bad news, and I dread to tell you." Thiery pointed towards the skeleton. "I think your best friend no longer lives, look ..."

Gimcrack turned quickly. Then, he began to laugh.

"What is it, why are you laughing?" Thiery asked.

"It is just that Staffsmitten is tall and broad in shoulder, and that skeleton is a dwarf such as I, we call him Whitey. He's an early warning system of my devising to surprise any unwanted visitors."

"I can tell you that he works rather well." Then it was Thiery's turn to tell of all his adventures.

Gimcrack leaned back in his chair with a redoubled grin and rubbed his hands together. "This is just grand. By now McDougal will probably have found out that you are dead, and when he comes to understand that you aren't, and that I saved you, not that I would brag upon myself to tell him, anyway it's a fact that only remains to be uncovered … I'll have done my duty and more in returning you to your friends, don't you think?"

"Oh, yes, and believe you me, I'll not hesitate to speak of your great deed myself. Then you can stay appropriately humble."

"Thiery, my boy, I thank God for the day that He saw fit to make you a friend of mine. Now, let's load our selves down with enough lamps and oil that we'll not end up stranded in the dark. If there's one thing I can't stand it's to be in the pitch blackness with thousands of pounds of rock threatening to squish the life from your bones.

"We'll be taking a lesser used under-street, an alley if you will, but we'll pass the main barrow under-road that goes all the way to Hradcanny. Strongbow has decreed that we must allow the priest-classes free use of the main barrow under-road and three of our main gate-ways, without escort or pass. So we'd best be careful not to be noticed. If there's one thing that gets me to shivering, it's those creepy, freaky, skulking, tattoo covered Dragon Priests. I just can't abide them."

They climbed down the secret stairs, and shut the door above them. Traveling for an hour through what seemed to be a man-made tunnel, about four feet wide and seven feet tall. Thiery was glad they'd brought plenty of oil.

Gimcrack explained that there were many passages of these dimensions, so that a dwarf could wield his weapons freely, but a full size man would be at a disadvantage, and a giant would be fairly stuck.

Soon, they arrived at a dead end. A huge boulder blocked the passageway. Gimcrack moved slowly, covering most of the lamp light with a cloth, and pressed his ear to a crack. "Here it is my boy," Gimcrack whispered. "We've just come out of a Beastie-free zone, but once we cross to the other side, there are trails enough to make your head spin. We'll also be crossing the River Sheol, not a nice name I grant you, and a number of canals. Over there, it is not a Beastie-free zone. So watch yourself. And don't stand too close to the waterways."

Gimcrack pushed against the boulder, and without a sound, it slid forward a few inches. Leaning down, Thiery could see that the door was a wonder of engineering design. It was set upon lubricated metal tracks, and once on the other side, a shelf of rock protruding from the boulder hid the mechanism from view. Horatio too, looked impressed, as his ears were raised, and his head cocked to the side in a quizzical way.

Sliding the boulder-door shut, Gimcrack covered the lamp. They listened for a few moments. Pitch black seemed to press in behind their eyes. With a great relief, Gimcrack uncovered a corner, illuminating a small area around him.

"I don't think there's anyone near," Gimcrack whispered. "And I'd like to give you a feel for the main Barrow under-road you're standing on. Get ready, then." He removed the lamp-cloth completely and turned the lamp to its full brightness.

Thiery wasn't prepared for the massive scale. Armies marching twenty abreast could fit along the level road, and an equally large river shone black on the other side, moving so slowly that it was difficult to tell which way it flowed. The far bank was raised a few feet above the water, forming a narrow ledge, a path of sorts, and directly across from them, even with the ledge, gaped a dwarf sized hole. The ceiling formed a symmetrical arch rising thirty feet at its center. Looking both directions, the tunnel wavered into shadows, and then finally disappeared into the black.

Gimcrack pointed at the hole. "That would take us where we want to go, but I'm not getting into the water, and there's a better way. We'll have to travel the main for a while though, so if we encounter anyone, and we've the time, we'll try to hide ourselves, if not, just keep your head covered."

But the road was empty.

Gimcrack had mostly covered the lamp again, so that it shone but a few feet before them. Occasionally, something in the water would stir; otherwise it was only the hollow echoes of their footfalls that disturbed the stillness.

Twice they passed flat bottomed boats. They had unusually high sides, with room for a rower and four or five passengers, but they were anchored on the wrong side of the river to be of any use. They looked like small floating castles. Gimcrack explained that the water-serpents could grow quite large, and one variety was poisonous, so the ferrys had to be fortified.

After a mile or so they came to a raised bridge, which was connected to a stone tower. The tower stretched like a fat pillar from floor to ceiling. On the far side of the bridge was another cave opening, four-men wide and twelve feet high. It was the under-road to the Hilltop Inn.

The tower didn't seem to have an entrance, but at about twenty feet up, there were four windows commanding a view in every direction.

Gimcrack tapped three times upon its base, and looked up. He shrugged his shoulders and tried again. Turning to Thiery, he whispered, "It's beginning to make me wonder that we've not seen any travelers, and now the bridge-works seem to be unmanned." Cupping his hands about his mouth he called out, raising his voice only a little. Still there was no answer.

"I don't like it," Gimcrack said, looking frantically about. "Not one bit."

The Chronicler

"Let me see, oh yes, Count Rosencross ... Count Rosencross ..." Diego Dandolo mused as he pulled upon his thin black moustache. He stood from behind the dark wood desk, one parchment perfectly aligned in its center, one ink well and pen with no trace of spill or blot, and a few scrolled papyrus and vellums stacked neatly in the corner. No dust, no mess.

"I am the Chronicler's assistant, and I assist in almost every particular, and I am particular about proper formalities. Since the Chronicler is now about two hundred and fifty years old—nobody really knows—since he is quite old, we have developed certain ... hmm ... how shall I say ... unconventional formalities."

Rosencross shuddered inwardly at the man's manner. He enunciated every letter with great care and exaggerated movement of his lips, as if he believed Rosencross was unable to follow normal speech. Rosencross had once seen a mother speak with her deaf child in the same way.

"Count Rosencross, I dare say you have something else on your mind, but please attend carefully to these very important instructions. As I was saying, some days he simply does not wish to speak, he's old, so I speak for him, and he watches the proceedings with an eye for detail. Details that I am familiar with and as I said before … am particular about. Do we understand each other?"

Without waiting for an answer, Diego Dandolo continued. "Excellent. Excellent. Now we have twenty minutes to prepare. We cannot rush an old man. But this room is beautiful, yes? And it is a good place to become acquainted. Now, this is very important. Please try not to make a sound, as I need all of my concentration."

He proceeded to walk around the desk, dressed impeccably in black with delicate white lace about the cuffs. Not a hair was out of place; it was all slicked back with oil. His leather boots creaked as new leather will, and a long thin sword hung from his waist. As he walked about the room, he dexterously moved the sword, keeping it from coming in contact with anything.

Kings and queens would have coveted the furnishings: plush sofas, pillowed divans, rows upon rows of ornately carved bookshelves, and yet one thing stood out in cold protuberance—a roughly cut stone bench. Diego paused and ran his eyes across its surface and then studied the Count.

"Yes, this is what it must be." Diego Dandolo spoke as if to no one in particular, bowed slightly, and waved his hand towards the seat. "A mighty maze, but not without a plan." He then walked, straight-backed, to his own seat behind the desk.

Rosencross looked at the other more comfortable furniture, and wondered if the man had intended him to sit upon the stone bench, and if so had he meant to insult him? The sun did not reach the spot from the windows, and no particular lamp shone directly upon it, but as he stood with some indecision, Rosencross noticed an inscription upon the stone.

Moving a step closer he read, 'When his heart was lifted up, and his mind hardened in pride, he was deposed from his kingly throne, and they took his glory from him.' Rosencross stood there as if transfixed, and then looked up at the strange man behind the desk. Diego was smiling pleasantly.

Just then a bell rang, issuing out from the door behind Diego. "He is ready for us, and he is early. It is too bad we had not more time to chat. Come then, follow me, Count."

The ante-chamber was decorated in stark contrast to the finery that had come before. It was not uncomfortable, but the furniture was rustic and sparse. A small fire burned upon the hearth. The Chronicler sat at his desk engrossed with some manuscript, his hand still resting on the bell.

Diego cleared his throat. The Chronicler looked up, as if in surprise. He was powerfully built, with some graying along the sides of his head, and more gray speckled throughout his beard. His singular feature was a set of bushy eyebrows. Raised, they would blend with his unkempt hairline; lowered, one could barely see his eyes peering through them. At rest? Perhaps when he slept, for they seemed to be in constant motion, accenting the expressions upon his face, and often one eyebrow would gad-about with no regard whatsoever for the motions of its twin.

He stood from his chair with the ease of youth, holding out his hand. He was one of the few left who had come from the other side of Babylon. He had known the great hunter Nimrod, and Rosencross shook his hand marveling at all the Chronicler had seen, all he must know. He would not do it for most men, but Rosencross gave a slight bow as the Chronicler sat down.

"Welcome to the Citadel!" Diego Dandolo exclaimed, startling Rosencross with his hue and cry. "The Chronicler bids you welcome."

Diego had positioned himself to the left of the Chronicler's desk and in such a way that Rosencross could not look at both men at the same time.

Why this invitation to meet the Chronicler, master of the Citadel? What exactly was going on here? Perhaps an interview. Whatever it was, from the moment he arrived, they held the high ground and kept him guessing—his flank was now exposed whichever way he turned—not that he expected a physical attack, but it had its effects.

He turned to face Diego Dandolo. The Chronicler became a blur at his periphery.

"Thank you, sir." And then turning back to the Chronicler. "It is an honor."

Diego stole behind Rosencross, appeared upon the opposite side, and once again startled him with his

oratory. "You are aware, that the Master is on the preci-
pice of retirement, he is old, so very old."

Rosencross glanced at the not-very-old-looking
Chronicler, whose eyebrows twittered. An amused snort
escaped his nostrils.

Diego continued, "It is our understanding that you
are the rumored favorite to take his place as master
here."

Now this, Rosencross had not known. Hoped, but
not known. He was an outsider from the outskirts of
the kingdom, but he had worked hard and given much
to gain Strongbow's favor, and this was very good news
indeed.

He bowed his head slightly to acknowledge the compliment. They seemed to be plying him for information;
he would try to keep them guessing.

"After the fair, our beloved Chronicler will officially
announce his retirement, and King Strongbow will then
announce the successor."

Rossencross kept his face impassive, but the news
sent his heart racing; he could taste victory at last. As
master of the Citadel, he would be in a most coveted
place from which he might become second in the land
only to the king. Maybe, one day, he would be the king.

"Of course, there are others to be considered, and
the performance at the games will mean much to the
people. Strongbow is ever thinking of the masses.
Curiously, some of your rival champions have not
arrived, yet there are only three days left. One, in partic-

ular is past due, a close friend of the Chronicler, maybe you have heard of him? The Lord Tostig."

What could they know? If Igi Forkbeard had not failed him, then Sir Tostig and his men would be in slavery now, and his pockets would have run over with the gold of it. Forkbeard said that they had all been killed by a great dragon, and so these two could not possibly know anything. Still, he had been hasty in dismissing Forkbeard. He could see now that it was important to remove all connections between himself and any wrongdoing—a dead man cannot tell his tale.

Yet again Diego Dandolo walked slowly behind him, the sword at his side brushed ever so slightly against the Count's leg. The man was becoming an annoyance.

"Indeed," Rosencross said, not looking at either the Chronicler or Diego. "Sir Tostig is one of the greatest of Paladins. I look forward to our engagement on the field above all others."

Diego was back upon the opposite flank again. The Chronicler's beard curved at the lips into a thin smile, but his bushy brows knitted together.

"The Master is pleased," Diego said. "He too looks forward to the contest."

There was silence for a long thirty seconds; it was thirty seconds exactly, for Rosencross counted as he waited for their next move.

One of the Chronicler's eyebrows raised, the other lowered. For the first time, Diego Dandolo stood at his side. He smiled pleasantly once again, and said that the Master—quite old—must rest now.

Diego acted as if he suddenly remembered something. "Oh, yes, there was one other thing. The Master has an abundant personal collection of works, but the library and science conservatories are his daily delight. It would be a great favor to him if we could continue to have access upon his retirement. If you are next in line, please consider this a petition to your good graces."

"To keep one as learned as yourself from the midst of academia would be criminal, sir. If I am the next Master, consider the doors of the Citadel forever open."

"Very gracious of you, Count, very gracious," Diego Dandolo said.

Still silent, the Chronicler smiled, caressed a book, and inclined his head towards the Count.

Rosencross bowed slightly again, and Diego escorted him to the door.

"I do love finery," Diego remarked. "I couldn't help but notice your gloves, made conspicuous by the warmth of the day, but very handsome. I do love finery."

It seemed a question would be forthcoming, but he only looked at him with an affable tilt of the head and smiled again.

The door shut slowly. Diego's face disappeared. Rosencross walked away, his mind convulsed in thought.

The Priest

There was a slight pressure just above his brow. He knew what it meant. He must relax. But as he walked the streets of Hradcanny—vendors selling their wares, a sea of faces, cobbled streets, stone and brick buildings—occasionally he would catch sight of a hooded red robe, and just as fast it would disappear.

The pressure spread to his temples and began to throb. He leaned against the corner of a building. In the nearby alley some boys were playing marbles. He remembered when he had played games like that, so long ago.

Beyond the boys, the alley opened onto another, less busy street. A flash of red again. Suddenly a man stood in the opposite entrance, robed, hooded. He pulled the hood slightly back: for an instant the light shone upon his face.

Him? Here? Why had he come?

The hooded Priest beckoned with his long fingers, marbled with blue tattoos. Rosencross felt helpless to ignore him. Passing the boys, the Count and his Priest—or was it the Priest and his Count—met halfway.

"Greetings, Count. Do our plans proceed as you would wish?"

"They do."

"Good, that is as it should be, for I have taken steps."

Rosencross hid his annoyance unsuccessfully.

The Priest laughed. "You were gone already, besides you would not have me slave to every whim of yours. What kind of counselor is he who says only what his lord wishes to hear, or does not act quickly for his lord's benefit? And I must listen to the Dragon first, yes? Come now, do not be offended, listen to the great thing I have done on your behalf."

His head throbbed now. He needed the Dragon Priests, and though he detested this one in particular, part of Rosencross was irresistibly drawn to him. "It is just my head again. Tell me then, what have you done, Priest?"

"In the last week we have cozen sacrificed one of the Dwarven Brotherhood. All that was found of him were some bones, his horse's saddle, and a shred of his clothes. Then there was my son, and now, possibly the greatest of the three, because of her innocence, her purity, and her faith in Noah's God ..." the Priest paused long enough to smile, a wicked triumphant smile that barely shown under the leading edge of his hood.

The heart of Rosencross beat heavily within his breast. He could feel each beat drumming through his temples—oh the terrible pressure—would his head burst or maybe his heart would harden and die. Yes, he had not done enough to protect her, and the faint promptings of his conscience, which had grown since he met her, now seemed likely to be extinguished altogether. Or the guilt might make him mad.

"Yes, my Count," The Priest said, laughing. "The slaying of the witnesses moves forward. That little girl's music will deceive her listeners no longer."

The ground swayed before him; Rosencross rubbed his eyes, and steadied himself against the alley wall. "I have taken rooms nearby. I must lie down till this pounding in my head abates." But when he opened his eyes the Priest was gone.

River Sheol

"Can't we lower the bridge some other way?" Thiery asked.

"Oh no, the chains are too thick to cut, not to mention the trouble we'd get in if we were to do such a thing." Gimcrack clutched his head and groaned.

"Why not walk further until we find another boat?"

"Yes, I suppose we'll have to do that." Gimcrack shivered, shaking his arm and leg that were nearest the water, like a child shaking himself out of his clothes. "It's just that, if there's anything I can't stand, it's water, and things of the water, like boats. They make me a little uneasy is all. I'd take a good solid bridge any day. Do you know what could happen if you were to fall in the River Sheol? Torn bit by bit, struggling to rise from the water, the weight of armor and weapons pulling you down, some serpenty-dragon-kind-thinga-ma-eaters gathering all around you."

Gimcrack was working himself into a quivering frenzy. Thiery calmly laid his hand upon Gimcrack's shoulder and reminded him that God was their rock, and their fortress, and their deliverer, their strength, in whom they will trust; their buckler, the horn of their salvation, and their high tower. Together they prayed, and while not tremble free, Gimcrack pulled himself together, enough to continue their journey.

As they walked, Thiery decided to praise and thank God for everything, knowing that this was most pleasing to his Lord. "... and I thank you for the watery depths, and the immense serpents and dragon-kind you've created. They are a wonder to behold my Lord, and they testify of your power and greatness and love."

Gimcrack listened in silence to the strange words, occasionally raising an eyebrow, when he suddenly burst forth, "His love?"

"I've been memorizing your friend Staffsmitten's book, the book of Job. And do you know that on the sixth day, when God made man, he also made behemoth, the chief of dragons. Actually, he is the chief of the ways of God, with a tail like a cedar. If you've not seen behemoth then you've surely heard of him. And then Job writes of leviathan, 'a sea-dragon so fierce that none dare stir him up, or stand before him. Out of his mouth go burning lamps, and sparks of fire leap out. Out of his nostrils goes smoke, as out of a seething pot or cauldron. His breath kindles coals. He esteems iron as straw, and brass as rotten wood.'"

"Yes, I can see why they testify of God's power and greatness, but where do you see love in those creatures, or in that scary river which conceals God's fearsome beasties?"

"Can you draw out leviathan with a hook?" Thiery asked.

"No, that's a crazy thought." Gimcrack laughed a little.

"Can you take him for a servant?"

"No."

"Can you play with him as with a bird?"

"No." Again Gimcrack laughed nervously.

"You'd agree then that none would dare to hunt leviathan. Shall not one be cast down even at the sight of him? Upon earth there is not his like… he is a king over all the children of pride."

Gimcrack was shaking his head. "I still don't see His love."

"Well, what keeps a man from coming to his Creator? What makes man try to be like God himself? What makes man think that he can speak out against his Creator?"

Gimcrack wrung his hands together. "Darned if I know. What is it?"

"Pride. It is to the humble and lowly of mind that God will look. So, God has shown great love towards us in giving us the vastness of the stars that no one can count, and the greatness of behemoth and leviathan to humble our pride.

"If God can play with the most powerful dragons as if they were a little bird, and yet they are so fierce to us, then how can we be prideful before our God? He has said about Himself 'who then is able to stand before me? Who has preceded me? Whatsoever is under the whole heaven is mine.' So, I think it is very loving of Him to help us see how insignificant we are by creating such fearsome beasts, so that we might humbly reach out to accept his grace, mercy, and love."

"I guess I never thought of that. You must spend a lot of time just thinking." Gimcrack unhooded the lamp a bit more, and peered at the glassy water.

The extra light showed a boat anchored not far away, and on their side of the river. "Now that's something we should be thankful for," Gimcrack said.

Horatio was the last to jump in, which sent the boat reeling from the river's edge. In a smaller craft with a steeper keel it might have capsized. As it was, this flat bottomed rower wobbled some and settled nicely.

But that's not how the boat's unsettling felt to Gimcrack. "Oh, God, save me!" He bellowed, throwing himself to the bottom of the boat. His nerves were shot, so Thiery applied himself to the rowing, and within twenty minutes they were back at the bridge and out of the water on the opposite bank.

Gimcrack kissed the ground, and thanked God with fervor. He turned to Thiery. "Now I have a sense for these things, and I'm sure we were that close to an all out serpent attack. Let's get away from here. The meeting time is drawing uncomfortably close. I don't want Lord McDougal to think I've run scared."

The new passage was similar to their first, except, it was double in size, and there seemed no end to the amount of smaller side tunnels that joined it. At one point they had to jump a trickling stream, and the passage changed altogether from man-made to a natural cave. It was here that they began to hear some squeaks, and a sound somewhere between a scratch and a click.

"What's that?" Thiery whispered.

"Don't talk." Beads of perspiration covered Gimcrack's face. "Just listen and be ready."

Horatio too seemed uneasy, turning at each sound. Once, two glowing orbs stared at them from a small dark burrow. Horatio growled deep in his chest, and then they were past.

Another hundred feet brought them to a large wooden door. Gimcrack knocked. The force of his fist pushed the portal open. There was a long drawn out creak. "It should be locked, and only the gate-keepers can open it. I don't understand."

They entered the room and barred the door. It was a circular chamber with a domed ceiling. At its center was a man sized hole, from which a rope dangled to the cave's floor. "That tunnel leads through the ceiling into the bridge-keeper's tower."

On the far side of the chamber was a large metal door; a thick timber to bar any passage leaned against the wall, unused. To the right, six or seven feet of slow flowing water passed under the wall, blocked off from the room by a metal cage. Gimcrack shuddered as his eyes passed it. On the other side was a cot lying close to a brick fireplace, a considerable pile of wood, and three wooden chairs encircling a small table.

"I don't understand where everyone is, there should be two gate-keepers and a cave-runner here."

"What's a cave-runner?"

"They're fleet footed men who run messages about Tump Barrows: important fellows." Gimcrack's countenance was more frown-full than usual and lines of apprehension creased his face. "I hope Staffsmitten is okay. He's gate-keeper for a lesser gate, a secret gate, so he's not bound to it day and night, as these men are supposed to be. But now I begin to wonder if some harm has befallen him, for I can smell trouble as clear as if I were that wolf of yours."

Thiery's eyes twinkled, as he thought that Gimcrack could always smell danger regardless of the odor. Still, he feared that Gimcrack might be right.

"Through this gate is a bridge spanning a smaller river that flows into the River Sheol, and a little ways further are stairs that rise for a good while, right into the Hilltop Inn's tavern. We should ascend those stairs into a hubbub of hungry customers just about the noon-hour, so we aren't likely to be noticed. Now, tell me if you've a better plan, but I say we pull our cloaks tight, raise our hoods, and walk straight as can be for the door. Once outside we make for the woods and our rendezvous with Lord McDougal. I tell you, Thiery, to see his face when he sees that I've brought you to him safe and sound, almost takes away the fear that's knotting up my insides."

"What about Horatio?" Thiery asked. "He's sure to draw some attention."

"Oh bother, I had forgotten about him." They both sat in silent contemplation, only to be interrupted moments later by the strange sound of someone whistling on the other side of the metal door—gateway towards the Hilltop Inn. The peculiarity of it was found in the perfect and melodic notes, vibrant and cheerful, which contrasted with the oppressive weight of rock, darkness, and unknown perils. Whoever they were, they must be of a virtuous and worthy character. Thiery could picture a warm fire, a room completely illuminated by light, an audience, captivated by the music and smiling up at the minstrel's face, sharing warm cider … it must be an altogether friendly bunch.

"Let's go and see them," Thiery said. "I recognize that song. It's one of the praises to the King of Kings. We could slip in and listen for just a little while before we leave. I don't think there would be any Dragon Priests there to recognize us. They don't like that kind of music."

"I don't know. It doesn't seem like the kind of place where a get-together would be held. See how we've put metal bars all around that water way, it's because of an especially large and fearsome serpent whose lair is somewhere beneath these rocks, and its underwater passage empties into the river beyond this gate. How people could relax and enjoy themselves when any one of them might be snatched up by the creature is beyond me. If you combine that with the mystery of our miss-ing gate-keepers, and I'm thinking it more than likely those priests are just a waiting for us, and somehow they know we're here, and it's some kind of devious trap."

As if on cue, Horatio's hackles raised and he lowered his head, lips pulled back in a silent snarl.

The water stirred, and just along the surface, the top of some creature showed thick and undulating as its front end disappeared under the far wall. Its body continued in length of twenty or thirty feet before its tail lifted out of the water, slapped the rocks above it, and then it too was gone.

"We must warn them!" Thiery tried to run for the gate, but Gimcrack locked his arms about him, whispering caution into his ear. They crept forward to the metal door.

Gimcrack hooded the lamp and carefully slid a peep cover to the side. Instead of the expected light from the adjoining room, there was only more blackness. Gimcrack lifted the hood slightly, first their feet and then the gate was given an eerie glow.

They could now see that beyond the peep hole was more wood. Gimcrack tried to open the heavy door, but it was as they feared. Someone had barred the gate from the other side, covering the peep hole in the process.

The whistling tune abruptly ended in mid chorus. There was a stifled cry, and then the sweetest, most pure voice Thiery had ever heard began to sing.

The sorrows of death compassed me,
And the floods of ungodly men made me afraid.
In my distress I called upon the LORD,
And cried unto my God: he heard my voice out
of his temple,
And my cry came before him, even into his ears.
Then the earth shook and trembled:

The foundations also of the hills moved and
were shaken,
Because He was wroth.
He bowed the heavens also, and came down:
And darkness was under his feet.
And he rode upon a cherub, and did fly:
Yea, he did fly upon the wings of the wind.
He made darkness his secret place:
His pavilion round about him were dark waters
And thick clouds of the skies.
Yea, he sent out his arrows, and scattered them;
And he shot out lightnings,
and discomfited them.
Then the channels of waters were seen,
And the foundations of the world were
discovered at thy rebuke,
O LORD, at the blast of the breath
of thy nostrils.
He sent from above, he took me,
he drew me out of many waters.
He delivered me from my strong enemy,
and from them that hated me:
For they were too strong for me.

The two of them listened in frozen anticipation, expecting at any moment that God would indeed come down upon a Cherub and blast the strong enemy with lightning, for the angelic voice sang with such fervor. Then there was another cry of fear, and then the song was taken up again, this time with a slight quavering in her voice.

With tears in his eyes, Thiery broke from his stupor and grabbed Gimcrack's shoulders. "We must save her, Gimcrack, we must! It is man's duty to save a maiden, but I am doubly bound to this one, for she's my sister."

"But the gate is blocked?"

"Is there no other way, no secret passage?"

Gimcrack's gaze turned upon the caged waterway, his body stiffened, his eyes went wide and almost seemed to shimmer with fever. "There is only one other way, but my heart will most certainly fail me if we attempt it."

Sweet Faith

Thiery saw that Gimcrack's heart might indeed fail him, or even his mind, and so, while he was only thirteen, he naturally took command. "Gimcrack, Gimcrack, look at me, I've got a plan. For it to work you must stay by the gate with our weapons ready."

That pulled him back from the abyss. "The gate? Ready? No water?"

"Yes, will you help me?"

"Yes ... of course ... I'll grapple with that creature, just keep my feet upon solid ground."

"Good, now tell me what to expect when I go under water and where to go. Once through, I'll unbar the gate, and together we'll face the beast."

Just then Suzie screamed. This time her singing did not begin again.

Gimcrack opened a small sliding portion of the cage. As Thiery lay down his weapons, all but his hunting knife, and removed his heavy woolen cloak and outer clothes, Gimcrack explained what he knew of the water's course. "This pool has no surface exit on the other side of the cave wall. You must feel your way along the left side to a hole not much bigger than yourself, and let the current pull you through, the channel lasts for fifteen or twenty feet. It then opens up under the bridge. Don't try and climb out on this side, it's too smooth and steep; you'll have to push to the other shore quickly so as not to go downstream. If you don't beat the current, then I shudder to think of what might become of you."

"Don't let Horatio follow me into the water." Thiery climbed through to the other side of the cage. Gimcrack opened their lamp fully and set it close to the edge. The clear water shown brilliant and clean against the first few feet, but then the light could penetrate no further. The blackness below and before sent Thiery's heart pounding.

Was the serpent or some other creature waiting just out of sight, ready to pull him into the deep? But there was no time to think of it, for Suzie needed him. "God bless us, Gimcrack."

"God bless us, Thiery."

And then the cold water enveloped him, as he jumped in feet first.

The shock of it almost caused him to take a breath under water. Instantly he felt very heavy and slow. When the bubbles cleared, he could see light above him, but nowhere to the sides. The light was growing fainter, and with sudden alarm he realized he was sinking, quite far, and still his feet hit no bottom.

His arms and legs felt as if they were weighted with armor; he wanted to stop and take it off, but his mind told him otherwise, and he forced his limbs to work towards the surface, towards the lamp.

He could see the shimmering light and maybe even Gimcrack's face peering down, but while he drew near, the current caused him to drift, and suddenly the light and Gimcrack's face were gone. And so was the air he so desperately wanted to breathe.

His mind felt deadened. What was next? Where was he? *'Please God, help me, I'm so cold.'*

The hole, yes the hole.

Though his mind revolted at the thought of reaching forth along the surface of the under-water cave, and in complete darkness, it revolted even more at the thought of finding and entering the channel. He knew that his hands were moving along the smooth rocky surface, but a numb bumping sensation beyond his elbows was all he could make out.

Something burned in his chest. It at least was warm, oh but it began to hurt, he would just take a little breath and relieve the pressure. Something warned him not to do it ... why? Why not breathe? Oh to breathe again. His mind was clouding over. So dark, so cold.

All of a sudden the water around him burst into brightness. The wet-fire? Gimcrack must have lit some upon the water. Just in front, and a little to the left was the round hole. He could reach out and touch it if he wanted to, but why would someone do that? Then the wet-fire began to funnel through the hole, and Thiery couldn't stand to be left in the darkness again.

He beat his legs hard, and suddenly the current pulled him into the channel. His arms lay at his sides, and there was no room to pull them forward.

Now the burning in his chest seemed to move towards his temples. They pounded sharp and loud in his ears. He would count to five and then take a breath or die. Each second his lungs tried to pull air from his throat, which caused a spasm of gulping at the back of his mouth, but still he refused to open his lips. But when he had counted to four he couldn't hold it any longer, and his mouth opened of its own accord.

The light was dimming some, spreading, and so with one final effort he pushed with his legs. Suddenly his arms were free of the channel. As his lips parted, air expanded his sunken lungs in a gasping rush, and the dim cave spun. He would have fallen from the dizzying effect had he been anywhere but prostrate upon the waters.

His mind was clearing again, and he remembered his purpose not a moment too soon, for the light upon the surface of the river was speedily disappearing downstream, it was indeed the wet-fire. Gimcrack had done well to shoot some into the water. Bless his soul.

There was just enough light to see the bridge above him, and the far shore, twenty feet away. He was being pulled towards that light. He almost followed it downstream, for his instinct wanted to keep it close. But the cold water was draining his strength and his instinct to be rid of the water, to feel the ground, to be warm, was greater—then he remembered Gimcrack's warning to make for the opposite shore as quick as possible. He also remembered Suzie's cries for help, and with it came the image of the great serpent coiling through the water.

Was it in the water still? Was it now, wrapping itself about poor Suzie? With numb, furious strokes, Thiery swam across the river, scrambling ashore at the far edge of the chamber. Although the light upon the water was now gone, there was still a slight glow. Candles burned on either side of a post at the center of the cave. Tied upright to the post, her head drooping, was the wilted figure of a girl.

The bridge was another twenty feet away, there Gimcrack and Horatio would be waiting, beyond the gate—weapons and reinforcement. He saw no sign of the serpent, so there would be time to free them.

He looked down at his frozen hands and noted with frustration that his right hand which should have been grasping his knife, was empty. And then he saw a slight movement, like the cave floor might be covered with a thin layer of marching ants or cockroaches. As he stared, unmoving, he realized with horror what it was. Only inches from his feet—almost hidden in the shadows—the huge serpent's scales reflected the dim candlelight as its length was sliding past.

Thiery was acutely aware of how defenseless he was; if only he had not dropped his knife. But as of yet the creature seemed unaware of his presence. He thought to let the serpent pass before running to the bridge, when his body began to shiver so violently, he began to fear detection.

He leaned forward, stepping high over the creature; only his front foot didn't act properly, quivering, it barely cleared the serpent's coils. His back foot moved more poorly still, and struggling to make the foot rise, it dragged across cold scales. Thiery tottered and fell. The ground slammed into his face before he could bring his hands forward.

He knew it should have hurt, yet it did not, and still more, it felt good to lie there. It would be so easy just to stay still, and sleep. Never had he felt so tired, so cold. But then he heard someone's voice far away, calling, and a dog, no, a wolf, his wolf, Horatio, barking, and then howling.

Somehow he was on his feet again; the bridge was before him. He stumbled across. Behind him he could see, or feel, or sense the serpent about to strike. Just before he fell again, he lifted the timber barring the gate, and slumped to the ground. A white, snarling form burst past, followed by a man, screaming unintelligibly. Then everything went dark. He could not keep the sleep away.

Back From The Dead

Thiery awoke to Suzie's fingers brushing ever so softly through his hair, and a smile, that warmed him as much as the fire crackling and the blankets piled upon him. Horatio lay at his side, and Thiery's hand was resting upon his head.

"I put your hand there," Suzie whispered. "I just knew it would make you both feel better."

Thiery put his hand upon Suzie's and thanked her. "Where's Gimcrack?"

She put her finger to her lips, and pointed. Upon a chair, which leaned against the gate, sat Gimcrack snoring, a bandage about his head.

"What happened?"

Suzie clapped her hands in her way, but without actually slapping them together, so as not to make any noise. Her face beamed and her body squirmed with delight. "Oh, Thiery, you men are so brave, and Horatio too. I just knew that God would send someone, only I never dreamed it could be you, seeing that I thought you were dead. And oh, you were right; Horatio is a most splendid wolf. Oh, and Gimcrack told me how you were poisoned, and it is just awful, and the dragons, it's so exciting, and I'm so thankful that God has protected you and given me my brother back."

Thiery had never been called a man before. He found himself trying to look more serious as he imagined a man should, but Suzie's excitement was contagious and he smiled up at her. "I'm glad that God has kept you safe also. Please tell me what happened."

After she explained about her change of circumstances from full time cook to Oded's helper, her singing for Count Rosencross, and her new guardians, she told of how the priests came for her in the kitchen.

"They told Flemup and Elvodug that I was needed in Hradcanny, then they swooped me up and rode off down the road on horseback, but they doubled back to the river, and would you believe it, there's a cave there, and the rest of the Count's men are camped beside the river. Well, they brought me down a passage, and tied me up to that post. I told them they'd better let me go, because the Count wouldn't like it one bit, but they only laughed. And then I said Oded would get them if they didn't let me go, but they didn't say anything else, except for some scary chanting which I couldn't understand. It sounded awful, so I started singing to God, and then they stopped.

"Well, then that big nasty snake came out of the water and slowly made its way around the room. Sometimes it would get close and so I would scream, and then finally it was too much for me, I'm just a little girl you know, and I guess I fainted. But not for long, because I was wakened by the loudest screaming I ever heard."

Suzie leaned forward, shot a glance back at Gimcrack, and then continued, "I thought it was a lady. Once I heard a woman scream like that when a spider crawled up her arm, but it was Gimcrack. Anyway, he was a scary sight swinging his mace in one hand and an axe in the other. He struck at the serpent something fierce, but then its tail swung through the air and plopped him right on the head. I started praying again, and Horatio held the serpent back while Gimcrack recovered himself, and do you know, he just started screaming again, and swinging, and looking … well … like he was crazy. And that big snake must have decided it had enough, because it slipped back into the water and disappeared, just like that."

Thiery looked over at Gimcrack with a tear in his eye. "He would have made Sir McDougal proud."

"Oh, yes, and there's still more. Then he yelled after it calling it a yellow bellied, armless beastie-thing," Suzie covered her mouth to stifle a giggle. "But then, as he came to untie me, four or five of those terrible priests appeared at the entrance holding crossbows and not saying a word. Well, Gimcrack was already trembling, and some blood was smeared across his face, and he looked kind of pale, but when he saw those priests he started to laugh like he had gone out of his head. In fact he was kind of scaring me. He said a bunch of stuff to them in between his cackles, but it was really hard to understand. Something about a horse, and God saving him from the grave, and how he was taking me with him into the under-world or something and they better not try to stop him, and the rest I couldn't understand.

"Well, those Dragon Priests looked unsure of what to do, and so he just started untying me. I thought they would shoot us any second, when you stood up on the bridge. You had been hidden in the shadows, and no one but Gimcrack knew you were back there, and you were deathly pale and bluish, and your white wolf was standing at your side. Horatio must have licked your face and woken you. When I saw you I was so excited that I called out your name. Then you staggered a few steps toward us, and those naughty Dragon Priests, who fill everyone with fear, finally got a taste of it themselves. They must have thought you and Gimcrack had come back from the dead to eat them up, for they ran away, and two of them even dropped their crossbows as they fled. But then you collapsed, and we brought you in here. Your skin was cold as snow."

"I feel warm now thanks to you and Gimcrack, but I think I'll just sleep a little more." Even before he finished speaking his eyes grew heavy, closing of their own accord, and in a moment he was sound asleep.

Thiery awoke refreshed, and ravenous, partly because he had not eaten for so long, and partly because Suzie had found the gate-keeper's pantry. The smells of her cooking sent his belly into hysterics. Suzie giggled at the sounds. "I'm almost finished; I've made some pan-cakes and tea for you."

Gimcrack too, stirred in his chair, and suddenly toppled from it. He rolled impressively to his feet, and blinking the sleep from his eyes, he stared about the room, his arms punching the air. Then he left them outstretched as if he might grapple a bear. Turning, he saw Suzie, Thiery, and Horatio gawking at him from the firelight. The confusion left his face, replaced by a growing red.

Suzie broke the silence by clapping. "Oh please do it again, that was very well done!"

"Yes, well, maybe later, little one." Gimcrack picked up the chair, and carried it to the bedside, the color in his face subsiding. "If there's one thing a man must be, he must be prepared. Thiery, my boy, it is good to see you looking yourself again ... what is that incredible smell? Goodness if there's one thing that I love, it's pan-cakes."

And so they blessed the food and made quick work of their meal. Feeling much better, they set their minds to the problems before them. The Inn no longer seemed a safe place to regain the surface, and in any event they had missed their meeting with McDougal. They would have long since gone to Hradcanny in search of Suzie and her kidnappers.

Though all were ready to see sunlight again, they thought it best to make at least part of their journey through Tump Barrows, and so they gathered their things and set off.

Once again on the main under-barrow road, the four of them walked on in silence, the meager light from Gimcrack's lamp un-shadowing a few feet before them.

Occasionally little Suzie's voice would try and brighten the hovering dark. She would whisper her thanksgiving that this was a 'beastie-free zone,' or 'another hour and not one Dragon Priest,' and her favorite, which was the only one to get a nervous smile from Gimcrack, was 'wait till Lord McDougal hears how you saved me,' and then she would look up into Gimcrack's face, expectant and hopeful that she was being a blessing to him. Thiery joined the fun, and soon the dark was not so oppressive.

Gimcrack was not so easily set free from his worries though. "If you must do that, please do it quietly. We're almost to the western wall of the Under-City, and we've still not seen a soul."

Gimcrack uncovered the lamp. Soon the tunnel swelled in all directions, unveiling a giant cavern with thick stone pillars rising to the ceiling. The Western wall did indeed have the look of a great fortress, with arrow slits high up and light shining from within, and in its center was a three-storied gatehouse, with portcullis and drawbridge. As the excited party crossed the bridge, Thiery peered into the moat, but their lights could not penetrate the black. Only a strange smell curled up from the depths.

The signs of life from within seemed to restore some confidence to Gimcrack. He patted himself upon the shoulder, and smiled down at Suzie. "See, I have brought you safely from the road, it won't be long now and we'll be well on our way to the surface."

They stood upon an outcrop of rock. The portcullis loomed before them. From one of the arrow slits above came a deep baritone, speaking with an almost musical oratory. "Gimcrack, maker of maps, and of things strange to behold. What is your business? And explain your young litter in tow."

Gimcrack got down on one knee, bowed his head and then rose again. "Cnutfoot, son of Redwald, I'm honored to tell you all that you ask. I have been in the employment of a certain Count Rosencross, master of two hundred soldiers, and special protector of Marduk's Dragon Priests. His priests initiated sacrifice upon me; this young man Thiery, and this beautiful child Suzie also. We all three were cozen sacrificed to their devil god, and I say now, the God of Noah, He saved us, and brought us together. I have given my pledge to Lord McDougal—unduly dishonored of the house of McDougal, and known now as McDougal, 'The Dead,' landless, but a man of honor—who God used to save me."

"Do you bring the priests of the dragon with you?"

"Perhaps they follow, but I don't know. We have kept our light covered until now, and we have walked silent-ly."

"Have you encountered any of the under-folk?"

"No, sir, we have seen no one. Staffsmitten was not at his gate, the bridge-keeper was not at his post, there was no one at the Hilltop Inn's gate, and we saw no one as we came here."

There was silence, and then a moment later a man of just under five feet, came striding forward beyond the portcullis. His girth was that of two men, and his arms and legs were half as wide as his body. His chest heaved under his armor. Long bearded strands of hair fell from under his helmet, ending at his waist. In his left hand he wielded a shield of enormous weight, and in his right, a great double edged battle-axe, as large as a giant's.

In spite of the weight of weapon and armor, he moved as if they were child's play things. Nothing of his person could be seen through it all. But his eyes were clear, piercing and true, and his noble soul reflected through them.

"Four of our gate-keepers have been found dead, six others struggle for life as we speak. It seems to be from some poison, and three of our runners have disappeared. We have seen no enemy, but we have heard that similar things have happened to the lords of the upper realms, those who were honest men. And so we have entrenched." At this Cnutfoot's eyes looked sad. "Do you know what this means, Gimcrack, maker of maps?"

"I do. No people, who are not of Tump Barrows, can enter the city. It is the Law." Gimcrack's head hung. He would not look at little Suzie.

"There is more to tell. The under-barrow road is no longer free from beasts. Someone has set Belcher free, and he has not been fed for three days."

Gimcrack's face drained of its color, his lips began to quiver. He tried to speak, but nothing came out. He just turned and looked into the far reaches of the cavern, then to the left and right. The young ones followed his eyes.

Suzie pulled upon his shirt, and when he glanced at her but for a moment, she spoke. "I trust in you Gimcrack. If God is for us than what else matters?" Gimcrack's eye began to twitch.

Cnutfoot turned sharply upon her, and then he laughed. "From the mouth of this child my soul has been stirred." Turning back towards the inner courtyard he yelled out for Baby to be brought forth.

In a moment the courtyard was partly filled with the bulk of a giant boar mount, the height of a small horse but twice as long, its tusks, head, and most of its body were covered in armor. When it spied Cnutfoot at the gate it ran to him, grunting spastically, and nibbling at Cnutfoot's arm.

"Baby and I will be your escort," Cnutfoot said, raising his battle-axe into the air, and kneeling before Suzie, his eyes sparkled as few people's do. "I know that the LORD saves His anointed; He will hear him from His holy heaven with the saving strength of His right hand. Some trust in chariots, and some in horses: but we will remember the name of the LORD our God." And then he winked at her.

The giant boar was looking through the bars of the portcullis straight at Gimcrack. As Gimcrack moved, so did the beady gaze follow. The next moment, with the sounds of chains tightening, the portcullis began to rise. Baby stuck her snout under the bottom-most rail and snorted, so that a cloud of dirt blew towards Gimcrack's feet. A whimper sallied forth from the place of groans and gulps within Gimcrack's breast.

Laughing, Cnutfoot stepped on Baby's lowered tusk. Baby lifted her head and Cnutfoot walked across the banded bridge of her long snout and nimbly turned to seat himself in the saddle. "Gimcrack, apprehension has never been written so clearly upon the face of man, and unduly so, for I discern that Baby has taken a sincere and sociable interest in you. Her name fits her well, gentle as a baby she is." As the gate finished its rise, Baby snorted and pranced like a dog before a walk.

Cnutfoot's eyes glinted mischief. "Though I do recall the time I dandied a babe upon my knee, soft and cuddly as my Baby here, and suddenly, it threw such a fit, it almost broke my ears with screaming. I was only too glad to give the dangerous creature back to its mother. I guess you never know. In any event if we cross paths with Belcher, you'll be glad she's with us."

Cnutfoot then turned his eyes directly into Thiery's and for the first time, Thiery could see just how alive with life and joy they were. Under his massive shielding beard, Thiery imagined a smile of such proportions that his face must be indelibly creased, fixing his cheeks like perpetual rosy apples. "How is it that you are so young, and yet you have all the trappings of a seasoned ranger, dare I say, the look of a beast-master about you too?

That is a fine looking wolf, and well trained for one which has not left off being a cub."

Cnutfoot's eyes suddenly widened. Looking at the dragon's claws hanging from Thiery's neck, he asked, "Can it be that you've killed yourself a dragon?"

"Not I myself, sir. Horatio, Igi Forkbeard and I were the only ones who survived the attack."

"And how many died?"

"Ten."

"How is it that you lived?"

"By God's grace sir, I was not on the immediate field of battle, but I was firing my arrows as fast as I could."

"I see. Did your arrows take any effect?"

"Yes, sir, again credit must be given to God, for it was very dark, and the creature moved so very fast, yet one entered its open mouth and another sunk deep into its eye."

"Indeed, that is well done. Then, young as you are, you have played the part of a man, and I should think a council of Rangers would be only too glad to bring you into their ranks quite soon."

"Thank you, sir." Thiery shuffled his feet, looked askance at Gimcrack, then at the ground, and then with bold resolve he turned back to Cnutfoot. "Sir, I would like to say something, only I'm not sure how to pro-ceed." And then the words began to tumble forth. "You see, sir, Gimcrack here, he's a most impressive fellow, and one of the best friends a boy could have. Twice now in two days' time he has saved me from certain death at the hands of dragon-kind. Why he even fought the great water serpent below the Hilltop Inn, saved Suzie, and faced off against four Dragon Priests holding crossbows on him. You can see the bandage there around his head where the serpent hit him. And he's been our guide through all of Tump Barrows, and I thank God that he's stuck by us so. That's all, sir; I just thought you should know."

Suzie, not able to contain herself at the heroic account, threw herself upon Gimcrack and squeezed him tight. Gimcrack's head was slightly lowered, but his eyebrows were raised. He was straining to observe Cnutfoot's reaction to the tale. Each time Gimcrack's eye twitched, his hand would start to rise as if he would force the eye to stop, then he would lay the hand back at his side in defeat, knowing the eye would not obey.

"A man can be beaten down and humiliated by other men—his heart grows to expect it and to fear it. That man's bravery in the face of his fears is to be prized, for the fear of man is a snare to the soul, and the fear of God, the soul's deliverer." Cnutfoot leaned down in his saddle, with an awkward tenderness from his callused hands he lifted the chin of Gimcrack and smiled with his sparkling eyes. "A humble son of the King of Kings … I'm proud to call my brother. Now let's see if we can't keep ourselves from Belcher's empty belly."

Cnutfoot crossed the bridge, and the rest began to follow. Gimcrack looked up at him for a moment, and then back at the dwarven soldiers who had watched from the gate, then to the faces of those who watched from the arrow slits cut into the fortress walls.

After the echoing voice of Cnutfoot ceased, and his gracious words still echoed in their hearts, Gimcrack straightened, lifted his mace in salute to the Dwarven Brotherhood of Tump Barrows, and took up the rear.

For three miles they traveled the main under-barrow road, when they came to a small path on the left. "Baby and I will not be fitting in there, and so with great pleasure I set you safely on your journey, may God bless and keep—"

There was not much of a warning. Horatio's head cocked, ears straightened; Baby's nostrils flared. Then a huge explosion of fire engulfed Cnutfoot and Baby.

Cahna-Baal

The road to Hradcanny, though short, was to hold two unusual incidents for Sir McDougal and his servant Fergus Leatherhead. Both would involve an attempt at rescue; both would be of great consequence and add a weight of responsibility, heavy upon them. The first encounter followed fast upon their departure from the Hilltop Inn.

In all the excitement, Oded had run off without Birdie, and Fergus couldn't bear to leave it without master or protector, so they traveled the road in search of Suzie with one more addition to their party. Fergus carried both the reins of his own horse and the spare mount's, along with his lord's shield in one hand. In the other, he carried a cumbersome bird cage.

"You are aware," McDougal said, with a hint of a smile, "as you have heard me say before, my personal effects are that of a hobbledy-hoy, that I ride a horse well below the ability of any lord, my lands are gone, my vassals and personal guard have abandoned me, and you, my truest friend, shield-bearer, epitome of valor and proper deportment, can barely hold my shield or sit your own horse because of some new allegiance—that not some great hero has won from me, but a tiny bird."

"Upon my honor, sir," Fergus said with a pained expression. "You lower yourself and elevate me too much. At a word I shall open the cage and let the bird free. It is only too plain that I have slipped in my duty. Please do not speak of it again, and in time perhaps I shall win your regard." With that, Fergus let the creature free before McDougal could protest.

"Oh dear, my friend, it was just a fribble, a whimwham, a trifling, a levity of no equivocation. Oh dear, I have lost you your bird for a mere jest."

And now both men wore an expression of intense chagrin as the bird flew off into the trees.

Both looked guiltily at each other as their horses trotted further down the way. Fergus thought on the duty of all the saints of God: to suffer long, to be kind, to not be puffed up, to not be easily provoked, to bear all things and to endure all things. Fergus had been prideful of his impeccable role as shield-bearer, and to hear it questioned sent him into a flurry of activity, not well thought out. How then should he proceed with McDougal, riding beside him, obviously chastising himself.

Birdie broke the awkward silence by alighting on the shoulder of Fergus.

McDougal held his breath.

Fergus sat straight-backed on his saddle, wondering if it was fitting or noble enough to ride with a bird perched on one's shoulder. "Perhaps the cage is unnecessary, sir?"

McDougal laughed. "It looks like Oded will have to get himself a new bird."

Fergus allowed himself a grin—for he did like the little creature, but of even greater import was that McDougal seemed himself again, joyful and free from guilt.

Soon after, it was agreed upon that Fergus should watch for sign upon the roadside, in case Suzie had been taken from the road. It was a more general search though, for too meticulous a pursuit would make them a day late for their rendezvous with Oded. But it happened that obvious trail sign was shouting to those who knew how to listen, so that Fergus soon called a halt. A great ruckus had occurred alongside the road, and most recently.

He searched the area, kneeling, prodding, and even smelling the earth. Handling some trampled grass, he at once laid his own foot alongside the markings of a bootprint, and then the measurement became his own cubit—finger tip to elbow.

After a moment he whistled, and breathed a deep sigh. "My Lord, there has been a skirmish here. No horses, but three at least of the giants, Anakims if I'm not mistaken."

"How do you know they are of the Anakims?"

"Since it is their particular fondness for torture, they will surround a man and widen their stances, effectively closing him in with arms and weapons outstretched until they trap him in an ever tightening circle. But by the look of it, whoever they got gave them quite a fight."

McDougal scowled, for the Anakims preferred a slow and devious torture. And if a Cahna-Baal was present—their priest of Baal—then they would eat the poor soul, believing they could inherit his strengths. The more noble and brave his performance during the torture, the greater the gifts bestowed upon those who ate of the victim's flesh.

No horses meant that they had not interfered with the Dragon Priests or Suzie, and she was foremost on their minds. McDougal's face became stony. His teeth grit one upon another. He peered into the heavens, and then they heard a barely audible sound far away, towards the mountain cliffs a mile or so from the road. It was a man in agony.

"Please, Lord," McDougal said, still looking to the sky, "keep my darling Suzie safe as we interfere upon this poor man's behalf."

And so, with Fergus tracking they rode carefully towards the towering cliffs in the distance. In silence they wound their way among pine, poplar, oak, and an abundance of gum tree; both men knew the danger they would encounter. The Anakims in particular were a fierce tribe, and it would be quite dangerous to steal a sufferer from their grasp.

As they passed a sapling gum, something caught their attention that was in strange contrast to their mission—two playful squirrels giving chase. First one, then the other, hit the sapling so that it bent far down towards the ground. When the first launched itself away, the gum tree snapped erect, and the squirrel giving chase shot through the air as if it were the ammunition of some great catapult.

McDougal paid particular attention and then began to note all the trees as they passed. Occasionally pointing, and then bending his arm towards the earth. Fergus, more used to his master's ways than most, couldn't help but wonder.

As they came to a knoll, quite close to the cliffs in front, both men dismounted, tying their horses to a fallen log. Climbing the knoll, again they heard the groan of a man in pain. The scene quickly became apparent as they gained the hill's crest.

There were three of them, all first-generation giants as it seemed, for they towered about twelve feet tall, with massive muscle and bulky chests. Each must have weighed five or six hundred pounds. One in particular was especially fearsome to behold, with his self-scarred body and his tonsured head. For it was the custom of the Cahna-Baal to cut their hair in a circle, and then shave the lower locks, though sometimes they would shave the whole head bald. His carefully manicured hair lay in stark contrast to the rest of his gruesome appearance.

But it was their intense interest in the sacrificial proceedings of Baal and their mistaken belief that the man they captured was in a place of honor, that caused Fergus the greatest fear and revulsion of spirit. They gave a salute of respect towards their sufferer's imperturbability, making careful preparations for small advances towards death, degree by degree.

Fergus wondered how man could come to such a place as this, from whence he first arrived, a tiny, helpless babe created in the image of God. All but Adam and Eve arrived in such a way. The first man and woman came without sin, but it was them that planted the seed of it, in each one of our breasts, and Fergus shuddered as he knew the seed of that depravation was in all men, including himself.

Fergus recalled to mind God's grace and mercy: 'Therefore have I hope. It is of the LORD'S mercies that we are not consumed, because His compassions fail not. They are new every morning: great is thy faithfulness.'

The poor sufferer lay upon the ground pulled taught in four directions, each hand and foot stretched by a rope and tied off to a tree or stake. Upon his bare torso were blistering red bubbles of skin, and still smoldering coals lay about his person where he had shaken them from his breast. His face was strained, and perspiration fell from his forehead and upper lip, despite the coolness of the day.

It was the Cahna-Baal's turn, scooping a coal from the fire with his knife, he flung it into the air, but with not enough arc, so that while it fell upon its target, it bounced from the man's chest and rolled a few feet away. The Cahna-Baal shrugged his shoulders. The giants watched in satisfaction, as their victim did not flinch.

McDougal whispered, "Do you remember when we were lads, and we fooled my mother with our play acting? She always thought you were especially good at it."

"I suppose." Fergus groaned inwardly, what was McDougal about to ask of him? A boy's charade was one thing, but that a noble servant of a noble lord should lower himself so... it was almost too much.

"You play the part of Rumploony. That'll put them at their ease. Best leave your sword with the horses."

Fergus replied with raised eyebrows, and an obedient run to the horses. Aware that he was dangerously close to mutiny within his breast, he called out to the LORD in his shame, begged for strength to serve as he should, and began to enter character on his way back.

By the time he reached McDougal, his face and hands were dirty, his garments were disheveled and soiled, his left leg and arm dragged markedly, and the left side of his face drooped. He added an occasional slurp, returning the drool to his mouth. But the greatest genius in his transformation was his infantile and addle-brained countenance, continually distracted by Birdie perching upon his shoulder.

McDougal looked at him with a start. "I say."

Two empty eyes stared back, and a curious, dolting grin.

"I say, you play the part of an imbecile better than I ever imagined, all that stoic self-possession of yours has been hiding another side of you just waiting the opportunity ... I say ... remarkable."

Fergus's fortitude began to waiver. But before he could shed his character McDougal stood up and marched down the hillside, arms, legs, and neck in complete disharmony. "Come along then, my dear Rumploony."

And so he dragged himself behind, bearing much weight upon his favorite weapon: his hickory spear.

The giants were so intent upon their purpose that they didn't notice McDougal's approach until he was sixty or so feet away, at which time, he pointed up to the sheer cliff above and called out loudly, "Oh, no, Rumploony, what are we to do?"

Fergus looked upon the cliff, but from the corner of his eyes he saw the great hulking forms jump to their feet. His vision at that angle was blurred, but it seemed that one of them was holding a massive tree studded with iron, and another held a boulder above his head, which looked as if it would be thrown at any moment. He desperately wanted to turn his head and prepare for the blow, but McDougal didn't, so he wouldn't either.

"The treasure," McDougal called. "How shall we get my treasure now?" He looked about the woods and cliff, and as if seeing them for the first time, McDougal threw up a hand, and strode forward to their camp, calling out the while, how fortunate an encounter it was. Fergus dragged behind, allowing himself to stumble and fall at one point, and then scamper after his lord.

Even McDougal had to crane his neck, looking up into their foreboding faces. Fergus let the drool begin, and waited for a profound moment to slurp.

"Gentlemen, Gentlemen," McDougal began, "this is most fortunate indeed. The tree is gone, some bluthering bad circumstances it is too, for up on that rocky wall: could it not be that I have placed my treasure? A tree to climb: could it not have been the only way of ascent? Do you see the ledge?" He made a grand display of pointing, and then pointing, and then pointing again, for the three giants wore a puzzled expression, though greed was the more evident. They shook their heads.

"I don't see it."

"I can't see it."

"I can almost see it," the Cahna-Baal grunted, licking his lips. "I can almost taste the gold." The three strained, and squinted.

"That is the genius of a hiding place upon the sheer face of a cliff, from down below, all we see are cracks in the rock. About seventy feet in the air, maybe eighty: could it not be an illusion, camouflaging a treasure trove of gold, silver, rubies?"

"Yes," the Giants announced in unified assent.

"If there be a treasure there, that I cannot get at by myself, nor with the help of my good servant Rum ploony." Here Fergus slurped, and the giants sneered in disgust. "But if I may attain it through the great strength of you brutes, then should not a treasure be shared with those who give the means for attaining it? If there is a treasure there, that is."

"Yes." Again they were unified, but no longer puzzled. Naked greed contorted their faces.

"I do not say that my plan will be easy, so what do you think of equal shares all around?"

The three giants laughed most wickedly. They looked at each other with what seemed to Fergus like knowing winks of planned duplicity.

"Agreed."

"Agreed."

"Agreed," The Cahna-Baal grunted. "And the plan then?"

McDougal patted Fergus upon his head, and at the same time he jingled the empty purse on his belt. "You shall have your sweet caramel pasties my dear Rumploony. These gentlemen brutes will help us to the means of getting them. Gather us some rope and three stout sticks of two foot length, while I tell the plan."

Fergus slurped, and dragged away to search about the camp, joyfully speaking of the Hilltop Inn's sweet pasties. This he added to the ruse to throw any future pursuit in the wrong direction.

On his third rambling pass near the stretched out sufferer, Fergus glanced back at the giants. Their backs were turned, absorbed with McDougal's flailing arms and rhythmic brogue. In an instant, Fergus severed the ropes binding the man's hands. He groaned slightly as the taught pressure was released.

Fergus looked up, heart pounding, if they discovered his purpose now …

Placing the cut ropes back into the man's hands, he laid his knife in the dirt and covered it with leaves. "Don't move. When the time comes can you run?"

He closed his eyes and nodded. Fergus returned to McDougal with the needed items. He caught the words triangulation, mathematical degrees of stupefaction, and engineering triumph, from McDougal's lips.

In thirty minutes, a most unusual and fantastical display spread before them, one that Fergus thought not likely ever to be repeated.

The tips of three young, but tall and sturdy gum trees were bent almost to the ground, each held partly by the strength of one giant, and partly by the configuration of rope looped and turned about a nearby oak. Still, their muscles rippled, and veins protruded from their necks and foreheads. They began to grunt for McDougal to hurry.

Another set of ropes were tied off between the three trees as a sort of net, from which McDougal was to be hurled by a giant gum tree catapult, seventy feet into the air, and land upon a ledge which Fergus was almost sure did not exist.

McDougal ran about the giants encouraging them, and checking for last minute tweaks. By the time he was finished, he sat upon the center netting which lay upon the ground. Rope lay everywhere in a confusing mass. The giants began to shake with the strain.

Surely McDougal would not stay where he was and be smashed upon the rocks. McDougal turned to wink at Fergus, as he yelled, "Let fly!"

All at once there was a tremendous din, a flourish of shapes, bodies, and trees, flying every which way. Ropes snapped, and pulled, and creaked. It was impossible not to blink and flinch, and still more impossible to tell what exactly was happening.

When the hubbub settled, all was silent, and time seemed to move incrementally slow. Fergus felt his heart beating.

He could not immediately grasp what it was he was seeing. He thought that he must have played Rumploony's character perfectly at that moment—staring dumbly for any sign of his master. Had he truly landed upon the still invisible ledge? Was there then also a treasure?

But why were the giants now hung upside down, bobbing limply, their heads bending against the ground and then straightening as the trees finished the force of their returning thrust? Only the Cahna-Baal was still conscious. A tirade of abuses rumbled from his speech.

In the middle of the spectacle, Lord McDougal sat calmly upon his launching net; a net that did not launch at all.

As McDougal was to explain later, he had only hung the ropes, which held the net, loosely within the branches, so that they simply fell away at the violence that ensued. As for the giants, McDougal had tied their feet to the bent trees, the final trappings finished when he checked everything just before the launch. The trees had not been strong enough of themselves to lift them very far from the ground, but the smashing, dragging, jolting journey they took had been enough to knock two of them senseless.

The man whom they saved had cut his legs free, and was gathering his stolen gear. He was a huge man himself, a bit taller than McDougal, and much broader.

He drew his sword and took a step towards the now defenseless giants.

"If we hurry," McDougal intruded his body between them, "we can be away before the Cahna-Baal has freed himself."

"If we hurry, we can make it so they don't free themselves at all," he retorted, raising his sword.

"I'm afraid we can have no part in murder," McDougal said, not unkind, but his voice carried authority. "In fact we would be obliged to intervene."

The man stared at the giants for a moment, his knuckles whitening on his sword grip. "While I don't understand your way of thinking, I'll not argue with the men brave enough to tangle with the likes of them on my behalf. I thank you and owe you my life. It seems that this is becoming a habit. My name's Igi Forkbeard."

Gazing upon them, he searched their persons most significantly. Suddenly his eyes went wide. "Where are your body charms, your idols; what protects you?" He paused. "Don't tell me you follow the God of Noah."

McDougal smiled warmly. "We do my friend, we most certainly do."

Queen of Heaven

As they neared Hradcanny, the extremes of God's creation converged in a breath-taking scene. Bog land and forest rose from the south, where the Black River wound its way to the sea.

Its source came from the mountains to the north: sheer cliffs, snowy peaks, and green valleys. Half of Hradcanny was situated on a plateau, called New City, nestled against the mountains. And half, called Old City, was built along a series of terraces that descended to the river port and bottom land.

Those who came by ship passed a great waterfall within sight of the city. The falling water careened from the side of a cliff into Knucker's Hole, and then to the river below.

The west was filled with grassy plains leading to an un-peopled dry wilderness. From the east, the direction from which McDougal's party now traveled, lay scattered forests, mossy hills, springs, and rocky outcroppings.

Along the highway Igi Forkbeard would not speak, unless obligated by questions from Lord McDougal, and then it was usually only a single word, from which he would sink again into deep reverie. His burns surely hurt, and his writhing upon the saddle confirmed it, but they had nothing to treat him with and lacked the time to gather herbs upon the hills.

The last leg of the highway dipped into a ravine, just as one caught the first glimpse of the city. Before the ravine was the monastery of Bacchus and the nonnery of Urania—Queen of Heaven; between them was the Tavern of the Seven Talons, and all lay cloistered within a high walled courtyard.

Here they were to meet Oded.

Upon this rise they paused before entering the open gate to look again at the city. Hradcanny's formidable presence set within so powerful a scene, showed its greatness in that it was not dwarfed by the imposing landscape surrounding it.

Just within the cloister gate was the grotesque image of Bacchus upon a pedestal, a wine goblet within his hand and a snake coiled about his leg. Next to his statue was a statue of the Queen of Heaven, beautiful and commanding above the courtyard.

Between them was a hole in the ground, and narrow stairs leading down to the crypt. To the right of Urania was a six-foot-deep marble-lined grave surrounded by candles, a pile of dirt along one side and a wood coffin on the other. Fergus felt a sense of foreboding, and thought it would be none too soon to shed themselves of this place.

They must find Oded and go.

Igi crossed himself and prostrated before the idols, and then stared dumbly upon McDougal and Fergus.

They did not bow, worship, or pray. They waited, sensing Igi might speak.

"You will offend them."

"They are nothing but stone and deviltry," McDougal spoke quietly.

Igi jumped to his feet, cringing before the statues, and then searching the faces of those around the courtyard who might have overheard. Without looking back at McDougal, he turned and hurried into the tavern.

Fergus sighed. They had left behind them a string of enemies. There was the witch Esla who had first pronounced the curse that unraveled McDougal's hold upon his land. And there were whatever forces that might be at work behind her, and behind the idea that McDougal must be dead by year's end—now only months away.

Aramis was back. How long before he was on their trail? And Rush. The pride and festering evil of that young man would surely drive him to retribution.

There was the giants whom they had fooled, and one of them a Cahna-Baal—wouldn't they too be a danger worth contemplating?

And now what mischief would happen here? And what awaited poor McDougal in Strongbow's court when he came before the Lady Catrina? Not physical danger—but still Fergus feared the encounter.

"Sir," Fergus said, as they tied the horses to a hitching post, "perhaps we should use a little tact in this place. There is just the two of us. Please take a care."

"I shall not shout from the rooftops, though indeed I'd like to, but I also must at times speak or suffer violence against the conscience that God has given me. Besides that, we may yet be three."

"Of course, sir."

Igi's powerful bulk sat in the corner of the tavern, his shoulders slumped. He stared at the table. A Bachus-Priest held out a goblet before him, and said something Fergus couldn't hear. Igi patted his belt pouch, then reddened; he stood up seemingly to leave.

"What is the problem here, priest?" McDougal asked. The three warriors stood around the priest frowning.

"He can't or won't pay the night-fee, so he must leave," the priest said, holding out the cup to them. His hands shook some. "And you too must pay. No exceptions. A copper if you please."

"What is this night-fee?"

"Master Squilby runs the hyenae and the Death-Hounds tonight." The priest laughed. "Anyone caught outside is torn to pieces. He doesn't feed them for a couple days and then they run in packs across the countryside. Master Squilby monitors the hunt from the air, carried by a great winged creature. Many people leave their farms for fear of it, and some come here for the protection of our walls, and our gods. It only costs them a copper."

"We three are together," McDougal said. Fergus handed the priest his money.

"The Queen of Heaven bless you. You may find an empty piece of grass in the courtyard to make your camp."

As the priest turned away, McDougal called after him, "And may the only true God, the God of Noah, bless you." The priest did not turn, but he paused, stiffened and then continued on his way. Fergus couldn't help but grimace.

They sat in the dimness of the tavern without speaking. A server came. McDougal ordered them a large dinner, for they were hungry, not having eaten since the morning meal.

Some inner turmoil fought within the breast of Igi Forkbeard. Perhaps his hunger outmaneuvered his pride. He took the food, but still he ate in silence. And then he pushed his empty plate away and asked, almost pleading, "I can't escape, it seems. I have no lord to follow, and no one to follow me. I don't feel as young as I once did. If I was to be your man, if you wanted me as such, Lord McDougal, would I also have to accept your one true God as you say?"

Before he could answer, a shadow fell across the table, and the men, distracted from their conversation, looked up at once. It was a lady, covered and hooded in the costume of the nonnery. Her body trembled, her brown trusses fell across her gown, but her face lay hidden. No hummingbird was ever as delicate.

What she said was so faint, it was uncertain if they had heard anything at all. Then she was whisked away by a tide of Bachus Priests and soldiers, out the door, and into the dusk of even. Before the door closed they could see torches lit, more candles, and nonnery mourners by the marble grave.

The possible sounds that teased into words, and played upon the chivalry of noble men, caused the three at once to stand and follow. Perhaps they had heard, "Please help me."

A crowd of sixty or so had gathered around the grave, yet still others shunned the spectacle. Some even covered their ears and looked away. There were those who knew it was an evil thing. The light of God still flickered in their breasts, but they were afraid, too weak to stand against it.

And so an innocent was to die. And part of them was to die with her.

The priest read from a book that none could understand. He held it above his head, almost screaming, "Does anyone dare oppose the sacred writ?"

All who beheld the proceeding watched with mouths agape, their faces pale. Torch and candlelight danced across them, across the ground, and licked up at the stone statues, bringing them to an eerie life.

"What does the sacred writ say?" It was McDougal. A moment before, the crowd had pressed against their small party, all wanting to see; now, suddenly, the heaving mass of onlookers melted away.

McDougal and Fergus stood alone.

Igi Forkbeard hovered near, but not too near.

The priest stared blankly, drool foamed at his lips. To quench his own conscience, and to open the way to the spirit world, he had partaken of some drug. His face contorted as he struggled to focus on the source of the intrusion.

"I say again, we can't understand a word of what you said," McDougal called out.

Still unable to see his persecutor, the priest jumbled his words. "Die ... law of the Vestal ... she must sleep, she die, she must die."

"I am a lord of this land, and Strongbow has authorized all lords as judges. Bring forth the charge against her, that I and any other lord here may judge whether or not she has broken the law of the vestal. If not, then place her in my care. I, Lord McDougal, 'The Friendly,' 'The Just,' 'The Dead,' have spoken."

There were over twenty priests whose countenances bore hatred at the words. Their high priest however, began to stagger. He dropped to his knees throwing up at the foot of the Queen of Heaven.

Despite the putrid mess, the queen continued to smile as if she did not see or smell the priest's hour-old meal. McDougal made a motion with his head. Fergus quickly approached the cloaked lady and held out his arm.

She reached out timidly and took it. Fergus could feel her shaking, as together they walked away from the open coffin, the marble grave, the idols, the flickering lights, the contorted faces, the astonished faces. They walked to McDougal's side.

In the distance, they heard the pealing of a bell. All heads turned towards the sound, towards Hradcanny.

The gates were now closed for the night. Dusk was lowering its final curtain. Someone in the crowd said, "The hunt begins."

God's Mercy

They chose a site close to the gate, placing their backs to the walled fortification.

"Fergus," McDougal said, "picket the horses over here against the gate. Make yourselves look as if we plan to stay the night, but have everything ready at a moment's notice to mount and ride. I don't know if they'll be trying anything for the moment, but when that Bachus Priest revives, I'm not so sure he'll let it go."

There was something familiar about the delicate lady that Fergus still supported on his arm. She held on tight, and though he still couldn't see her face, he could hear her sniffles. Her narrow shoulders hunched even closer together. It was too much. Everything in him said she needed someone to comfort and hold her.

But that could not be: two strange men, now her protectors, could not take such liberties. Fergus looked questioningly at McDougal.

McDougal's heart shown in his face. He shrugged his shoulders, lifted an arm as if to pat her on top of the head, hesitated, and patted his own cheek instead. He stumbled for the right words. "Oh dear, well um … dismal, freaky, scary, a heart-sinking mortal funk, really a downright hurlothrumbo of an alarming program they have going on here. I can see why you aren't feeling so great little lady. I mean if you are wanting a nice place to be buried, anywhere is better than here."

She gave a small laugh amidst a sniffle. She spoke shakily, interrupted by quick intakes of breath, but there was an evident smile in her voice. "You have always been most becoming when you do things like that."

McDougal's half raised arm, hung in the air as if he rested it upon some invisible branch. His body bent far forward towards the young lady, and his expression which normally would have caused Fergus to be embarrassed, now made him smile. For Fergus had figured out who the lady on his arm was; and he knew that she would always be graceful towards McDougal's singular behaviors.

McDougal managed an awkward bow. "I'm afraid you have me at a disadvantage. I cannot see your face, nor recognize your voice, yet you address me with no formalities."

"Oh, McDougal." She giggled as she curtsied. "This is fun." Then she pulled back her hood, and smiled, a little sheepishly, tears still wet upon her cheeks.

"Mercy ... but how?"

"Princess Catrina, for that is what I am to call her now, thought it best if I were not so much in her way. So she asked Uncle if I would not be better suited as a Vestal Virgin for the Queen of Heaven."

"But you were her special attendant, cousins, and still more I thought you close friends."

216

The tears brimmed upon her eyes, making them shine. "I love her so, but she has changed much since you've seen her."

"You have changed much while I've been away; you've turned into a lady. Fergus was right when he said I'd not be tossing you in the air again."

There was an awkward moment. Fergus tried his hand at smoothing things a bit. "You followed McDougal like a puppy, my lady, but now you've grown into a .... a ... I mean to say, not a dog... a beautiful lady."

Mercy flushed, looking away from McDougal to Fergus. "Yes, thank you Fergus, an apt metaphor."

"You're too kind, my lady." He was glad of the darkening night which hid some of the color in his cheeks. Why was it suddenly warm? He used to speak so easily with Mercy. Now it was difficult. Well, best to keep his mouth shut. It was not a servant's place to speak so familiar like with a lady.

McDougal changed the direction of things. "But why did Strongbow send you here? I thought he served the truth, and Catrina too."

"He would not look at me as he told me where I was to be sent, only that it was a great honor, and that my father would have been pleased. He has counselors whom I fear. I tremble even to be in their presence—they whisper things in his ear. Catrina openly follows the gods now, and I think that she dabbles in the forbidden arts. She tired of my voice calling her back."

"How can this be? But was your death part of their intention? Otherwise how dare these priests treat the king's niece so?"

"Oh, I do not think that possible. It is just that they think I have broken the Vestal Laws, and their gods require live burial to atone for the sin."

"But have you joined their order?"

"Not willingly, it was by the king's order, and so I am here."

"Please do not be insulted by my question, for I would never doubt your own purity, but can you tell me why they think you have broken the Vestal Law?"

"I escaped. And I was gone for five hours before they captured me. Five hours without an escort. The law then assumes infidelity against their god. And so I am branded as adulterous."

"Nonsense!" McDougal shook angrily. "Let God be true, and every man a liar. Just last night I bowed my knee before a young girl, and we vowed to be her protector. She's been stolen away, and we seek her now. I bow my knee before you also Mercy, and ask to be your protector too, may God give me the strength and wisdom to carry the duty with honor. There are only a few of us. If you accept, I know it will make all our hearts glad, especially Suzie."

"You know I accept you, Lord McDougal, there is no other besides my father whom I feel safer with."

He rose from his knee smiling. He seemed bigger, stronger. Fergus thought then, this is the kind of thing

God made McDougal for; the more he lays down his life for others, the greater a man he becomes.

"There is one more thing," McDougal said, serious again. "Maladroit, unwieldy, bumbling, graceless, ungainly, gawky ... these are just some of the words used to describe myself. You remember me perhaps more through the rosy colored eyes of your childhood. I suppose I thought you should be warned. I would hate to invite shame upon your fair countenance or in your heart."

Mercy's eyes shone brilliant again. She left Fergus's arm to touch the gangling hand of McDougal. "Nonsense," she said. "Let God be true, and every man a liar."

Igi Forkbeard approached the camp and saw an extra place had been laid out for him; he relaxed some. "I've been walking amongst the people and listening to their talk. The Bacchus Priests, but especially the nonna, stir them up. They say the gods will be angry, and the night of the hunt is a bad night to offend them. They've removed the high priest and his mess, and they've lit the candles once again that lie about the grave."

"Well done, Igi Forkbeard. To answer your question from earlier, no you do not have to believe the way we do, but do not be surprised if we try to make a believer out of you. You are my man then, and now we are four strong, for when Mercy was only fifteen she could shoot ten arrows per minute and not miss her mark. And she's had three years to improve. Well then, we've not enough horses, so you'll have to ride behind me, Mercy. I don't have to tell you to hold on tight. If we must, we can take to the trees, though I'd hate to leave our horses to the hounds."

In thirty seconds they'd gathered their things. "Open it!" McDougal commanded the guard upon the wall.

"It's against the rules to open after dark."

"They're coming," Mercy whispered.

The Bacchus Priests and a crowd of lay people carrying assorted weapons were gathering courage. The nonna began their lamentations at the grave.

McDougal motioned to Fergus as he spoke. "We hate to get in the way of a man's duty, but we've got a lady to protect, and if we're not on the other side of this gate in five seconds, I'll have no choice but to shoot you full of arrows. It's a pity they don't arm you with a shield up there."

As McDougal spoke, Fergus climbed to the top of the ladder, and when McDougal drew his bow back, the soldier ran along the parapet to gain the cover of a bend in the wall. Fergus pulled himself up and released the upper gate locks. Igi removed the timber that barred the doors. In a moment they were through.

The crowd rushed forward, not to give chase, but to close and bar the gate once again. Fear of the hunt was upon them.

Fire Belcher

Belcher had been lying in wait on the opposite side of the cavern, perfectly still in the dark, and so Baby and Horatio hadn't sensed the great predator in time to give warning.

Just before Belcher's fire had engulfed Cnutfoot, Horatio had tensed, and Thiery, as a fledgling beast-master, was learning to mind his wolf. His fingers were on an arrow in an instant.

From within the flames Baby squealed, sounding more like a farm pig than a war mount. Cnutfoot roared his battle-cry; but it was cut short by a groan.

When the flames disappeared as quickly as they had come, only two meager lights remained burning—someone still held a lamp, and Cnutfoot's beard was aflame. There were sounds of a struggle.

Cnutfoot fell to the ground, rolling, and rubbed his face into the dirt.

There was a moment when all else was terribly dark, for Thiery's eyes needed time to adjust from the previous brightness. Sound was strangely muted even as the pandemonium of battle accelerated around him.

A large form loomed to his side. Thiery checked his arrow just in time, almost firing into the side of Baby.

He could hear Horatio snarling off to his right, but there was no sight of him. Thiery noted Gimcrack hurrying Suzie to the entrance of the side tunnel. She at least was safe.

Then the creature came into view, double the size of the boar-mount and thick everywhere. Reddish-brown skin stretched over a fat bulbous head, with no noticeable neck. Its middle bulged out the sides of its stubbed legs and almost touched the ground as it moved, and massive claws scratched like sixteen shovels striking the earth.

A single horn jutted from its snout, longer ones shot back from above each eye like curved sabers, and its tail twitched as if ready to strike.

It was.

Cnutfoot had dropped his shield and still knelt in the dirt when he saw Belcher's mouth opening before him. Cnutfoot rolled; the snapping jaws closed inches from his smoldering body.

Again the jaws snapped, and again Cnutfoot rolled.

Three arrows stuck deep into Belcher's side. Thiery continued to fire as fast as he could work his fingers.

Horatio harried at its tail.

But the dragon was intent only upon the fallen warrior. Then there was a rumbling of hooves, like the thundering of a chariot race. Baby tore down upon them in a fury of screams and snorts.

She collided into the fat dragon belly, lifting Belcher off his feet for a moment. Then they tumbled into a snarling mass, distorted by the shadows beyond the one lamp that still burned.

Gimcrack gathered Cnutfoot's shield and battle-axe, and all ran to the safety of the smaller cavern—all but the wolf.

Where was Horatio? Thiery felt a growing dread. In less than a week, Thiery's heart had grown so close to the wolf that he felt as if he would burst into tears at the thought of losing him. Oded had told him that each animal he trained would likely die in battle or at least they would die before Thiery, even if it was from natural causes. So he was to prepare himself for the unhappy event, but it didn't seem to help.

Thiery whistled over the din, again and again, until suddenly Horatio burst from the dark edges and ran to his side. Thiery sent his thanks heavenward.

Cnutfoot's body was blackened, but his eyes still shone joyous. His beard was almost gone; it seemed what was left had almost melted against his face.

"Go now," he shouted. "Baby and I will take care of Belcher. Gimcrack, quick, strap my arm to my shield, tight. I'll have no disobedience from you either, when I turn my eyes back to this tunnel, you'd best be long gone. I'll make a run for it myself, but upon Baby's back and I don't want to worry about what's become of the three of you. Leave that lamp lit by this spot, so it'll not be knocked over."

And so he ran back into the fray. The last thing they heard was Cnutfoot's melodious baritone cheering Baby to the fight.

"All I've got left is this torch," Gimcrack said. "It should give us an hour's light, but two is what we're needing, so we'll have to move fast. Come now children; let us raise our voices to heaven. If we cannot fight alongside Sir Cnutfoot, we'll stand by him in our prayers."

Suzie smiled at them both. Thiery could see the weariness in her, but she didn't complain. He could also see that she'd never keep up with the pace Gimcrack subscribed, and then they'd be in complete darkness. He shuddered.

Scooping her up, Thiery set her on Horatio's back. "Can you hold on? Grip tight. It won't hurt Horatio, he's a tough one."

She did not answer, but dug her fingers into Horatio's hair, and laid her head upon his neck. She soon showed signs of further fatigue, and so Thiery helped to steady her. After twenty minutes of hard running, her hands went limp, bouncing against Horatio's forelegs.

A picture shot before his eyes of Gimcrack asleep against the Hilltop Inn's under-gate; himself, lying upon the bed, unable to keep his eyes open; and Suzie watching over them both. Looking back, he could see just how tired she had been, yet she had stayed awake. How long had she been awake?

"Gimcrack," Thiery called. "Suzie's fallen asleep. Can you help me keep her from falling?" And so they ran on either side of the wolf, one hand each upon her back, the torch beginning to flicker, and the sides of the cavern knocking against their shoulders—three abreast being too much for the tunnel's width. But the scrapes and bruises were nothing when compared to the honor of protecting their little friend.

The torch flickered for the last time and plunged them into a black so thick it crawled into the crevices of their clothes, under their eyelids, and into their mouths. Gimcrack groaned. Thiery imagined Gimcrack's eye twitching, and the poor man not able to find his own face to press against it.

"Don't worry about the dark," Thiery said. "You're a map maker; you can bring us the rest of the way."

"I can't stand the dark. If there's anything above everything that I can't stand, it's the pitch dark with no hope of light. I'll never get us out now."

"Listen. We ran hard, it can't be far."

"Yes, we are close, but we've just come under Hradcanny, and the passages multiply, I'm more likely than not to take us further afield. I grew up on the stories of those who wandered the caves without ample supply of light and got lost. Some were never found, some went mad ... and don't you know what all cities carry with them? Vermin, crawling beasties, and worse —"

"Gimcrack, sir, you'll not get us there thinking on every danger. It is true that God may allow us to die down here, but I can tell you that if I was alone I'd not likely make it, and this dark is bearable because of your presence. I'm thankful that you are a gift from God for me in this fearful place. And what about Suzie, would she have come through without our hands guiding and protecting her?"

"No, I dare say no."

"We are God's gift to her. And as far as beasties go, we're no match for much of anything in this dark, but aren't you comforted by Horatio's presence on that account?"

"Yes, that is true."

"And God already knows everything that will happen to us today. He knows my down-sitting and mine uprising, He even understands my thoughts afar off."

"Tell me more, young Thiery, these words comfort me."

"He is acquainted with all my ways. For there is not a word in my tongue, but, lo, the LORD, He knows it altogether. He has beset me behind and before, and laid His hand upon me."

Gimcrack sniffled. "Oh that is beautiful stuff, just like we're doing for the young lady here by laying our hands upon her back. Please keep on."

Thiery too, felt the heaviness of the dark creep back out of their clothing, and so he spoke more of the glorious intimacy of their God. "Such knowledge is too wonderful for me; it is high, I cannot attain unto it. If I take the wings of the morning and dwell in the uttermost parts of the sea; even there shall thy hand lead me, and thy right hand shall hold me."

"Those sound like the very words of God," Gimcrack whispered. "The very words."

"If I say, surely the darkness shall cover me;" Thiery paused and then answered, "even the night shall be light about me. Yes, the darkness hides not from Thee; but the night shines as the day: the darkness and the light are both alike to Thee. How precious also are Thy thoughts unto me, O God! How great is the sum of them! If I should count them, they are more in number than the sand."

"Now I've got the shivering chilblains. If God thinks that much about us, then I ought not to fret so. What's that thing you say again ... I'll do my best with one eye on the task at hand and one eye upon my God." Then he chuckled. "Only I can't see a darn thing."

And so they continued for over an hour, with Thiery encouraging Gimcrack, and Gimcrack ever tottering back towards the brink of fear, yet never falling into its clutches.

Suzie was startled awake by sudden sobbing. Thiery could feel her body tense and half rise from her perch upon Horatio's back.

Thiery called out to Gimcrack, "What is it? What has happened to you? Are you okay? Please answer." Gimcrack only cried the harder along with some blubbering nonsense.

Then Suzie cried out, "Have I gone blind? I can't see anything."

"No, sweet sister. It is just that our torch has burned out."

"What's wrong with poor Gimcrack? I think I shall cry too, he sounds so broken and it makes me feel very sad."

Gimcrack stopped as quickly as he had begun, only a few sniffles, and then he spoke so that one could hear his smile. "I am sorry, children, truly I am. It is just that I have found the hidden stone that unlocks our passage. God's goodness has overwhelmed me. I do not cry for fear or pain, but from thanksgiving and wonder that He should help such a faithless wretch like me. Stand back now."

They could hear the grating of stone upon stone, and then faint light streamed in, but to them it was glorious and shining.

Stepping through to a small landing, Gimcrack swung the portal closed, and they ascended a flight of stairs, which opened upon a narrow passage. Here they had to crouch and travel single file for a few yards.

Light streamed through a black metal grate in the tunnel's ceiling.

Gimcrack pushed against it with his head—ever so slowly. It opened without a sound. He peeked into the room above. "It's all clear, but you can't be too careful. This is one of my favorite places, and we shall call it home until we've found Sir McDougal and the others. Come now and enjoy dwarven hospitality in one of our way-stations."

Standing straight, with his feet still on the passage floor, the grate hinged back, and his shoulders broke free into the chamber above.

Climbing out, he turned and lifted Suzie. Thiery pulled himself through, and then Horatio followed with a scrambling leap. They stood at the mouth of a large hearth, from which the black grate now seemed only to be the entrance to an ash pit.

Suddenly, Thiery realized he was hearing a tumult of unusual sounds. The buzz of voices, cart wheels rolling on cobbled streets, a donkey braying, and a child crying in the distance. It was the sounds of a city, the sounds of Hradcanny.

They stood on the bottom story of an abandoned stone tower. The floor was littered with broken beams and the remains of crushed furniture. Lower window-slits were filled in with rubble and mortar, and a heavy door stood upright on the ground—its hinges rusted off—but still held in place by nails and planking.

A circular stair wound its way along the perimeter, higher and higher into an increasingly bright world, for the occasional windows on the upper tiers were open to the outside.

"Oh dear," Suzie gasped and looked at Gimcrack. "I suppose it just needs a little cleaning. But I can see its potential, really I can."

Gimcrack laughed. "No, this isn't it. We still have to climb the stairs. Wait till you see the view. We should hurry though. It will be getting dark soon, and I want you to see it in the day. But we'll also have a full hunter's moon tonight, and that shall be beautiful too. The stairs are somewhat old so let's space ourselves a bit, not that

I'm worried about them giving way, mind you, just a precaution. I always say you can't be too cautious."

They climbed eighty feet of creaking stairs and emerged into a comfortable room with many sleeping packets, a large table, some chests, and another stair leading to the rooftop. It was clean and cheerful.

"Quick now, up to the roof."

A bell rang out.

Then another. Soon the city sounds were drowned in a clanging ambuscade of bells.

They froze upon the steps leading to the roof-top. Thiery shouted over the noise. "What is happening?"

Gimcrack answered by raising his finger to his lips.

Suddenly the bells stopped, and for a few minutes, the sounds and activity of the city were hushed, expectant. Thiery and Suzie looked about them wondering what terrible thing might happen next.

"It is the hunt," Gimcrack whispered, as they climbed out onto the tower's parapet. "The hyanae and the Death-Hounds will be out tonight. I should have known because of the full moon."

The tower was part of the inner curtain wall of the Old City—set on the crest of the plateau. New City extended for half a mile further, on a slight decline, which made the old wall and many of its towers obsolete.

They crossed to the battlements and peered out. The view was incredible. Towers and spires rose to precipitous heights. Wide, symmetrical streets were crisscrossed by waterways, with all kinds of gondolas and water-taxis selling transportation or merchandise. There were temples, storefronts, markets, homes, and a huge arena for the games. New City dazzled with wealth.

In contrast, looking down the terraces of Old City, they could see that the streets were narrow and crowded with the poorer classes and their litter. There were pockets of wealth, but mostly it seemed a perilous place where one might be assailed by pickpockets, ruffians, or disease.

The glory of Old City was its port and the Citadel.

The glory of New City was its popular arena and New-Castle which overlooked it.

The Citadel had walls that were eight feet thick; New-Castle's walls were twelve. The Citadel's highest towers climbed to one hundred feet; New-Castle's sought the clouds at one hundred and sixty. The Citadel was without a moat; New-Castle's moat was thirty feet wide and filled with poisonous serpents. The Citadel was undermined by hundreds of passages and secret tunnels which joined to Tump Barrows and other places within the city; New-Castle, built by Strongbow, was purported to have no such deficiency in its security. And the list went on and on.

Milling about upon rooftops and towers, gatehouses, and battlements, the cities' populace strained their eyes eastward. The light of dusk never left, for the moon shone, caressing the eastern plateau with its milky haze.

Thiery looked beyond the city walls, down the main road of Hradcanny. It reflected gray as it cut through the low waving grasses, stark and lonely with no buildings or trees to accent the land, before it dipped down into a valley, and then back up again where the cities' inhabitants could see the lights of the Bacchus and Urania cloister and mouse-sized people scampering within its fortifications.

But then, they could also see, in fact the whole of Hradcanny could see—three horses with riders, and they on the wrong side of the cloister gate.

The people of Hradcanny rent the air with a collective gasp.

"What will they do?" Suzie asked, clinging to Gimcrack's side.

"If they flee now, and their horses are rested, then just possibly, they might escape. But if they stay where they are, then they will die."

"Why don't they go back inside that little fort?"

"Once the bells have tolled, they'll not open their gate for anyone. If the beasts got in there, then it would be death for them all, and well they know it."

"Will no one help them?"

"Oh no, the hyenae and the Death-Hounds and Master Squilby are part of the defense of our city. To help those people would mean to attack our own defenses, and it would be looked upon as a crime."

"Can they not help themselves then?" Thiery asked.

"Assuredly so, but sixty to eighty hyanae, at least ten mounted Death-Hounds, and Squilby directing them from the air ... it would be over before you could blink. Don't worry. I'm sure they will run for it."

The three horsemen did not run away though. Instead they turned their steeds onto the Hradcanny road towards the city, and down into the valley, out of sight from the city walls. Again there was a gasp from Hradcanny, as if the city itself were alive, astonished at what it had just seen.

Then silence: a bating of breath.

A moment later Hradcanny's central gate opened its iron barred mouth, and the beasts of the hunt spewed forth in waves of gnashing teeth—crooning their death song.

The Gospel of Jesus Christ

JESUS CREATED US:

Revelation 4:11 *(see also Col. 1:13-17)*
Thou art worthy, O Lord, to receive glory and honour and power: for thou hast created all things, and for thy pleasure they are and were created.

JESUS REDEEMED US:
(set free, to save from a state of sin and its consequences)

Revelation 5:9
And they sung a new song, saying, Thou art worthy to take the book, and to open the seals thereof: for thou wast slain, and hast redeemed us to God by thy blood out of every kindred, and tongue, and people, and nation.

SAVED FROM HELL
AND THE LAKE OF FIRE:

Revelation 20:11-15
And I saw a great white throne, and him that sat on it, from whose face the earth and the heaven fled away; and there was found no place for them.
And I saw the dead, small and great, stand before God; and the books were opened: and another book was opened, which is the book of life: and the dead were judged out of those

things which were written in the books, according to their works.

And the sea gave up the dead which were in it; and death and hell delivered up the dead which were in them: and they were judged every man according to their works.

And death and hell were cast into the lake of fire. This is the second death.

And whosoever was not found written in the book of life was cast into the lake of fire.

NEW HEAVEN AND EARTH
ETERNAL LIFE:

Revelation 21:4 *(Read Revelation chapters 21 and 22)*
And God shall wipe away all tears from their eyes; and there shall be no more death, neither sorrow, nor crying, neither shall there be any more pain: for the former things are passed away.

HOW DO WE ESCAPE HELL
and RECEIVE HEAVEN?

1 Peter 1:23,25
Being born again, not of corruptible seed, but of incorruptible, by the word of God, which liveth and abideth for ever....
But the word of the Lord endureth for ever. And this is the word which by the gospel is preached unto you.

2 Timothy 3:15-16
And that from a child thou hast known the holy scriptures, which are able to make thee wise unto salvation through faith which is in Christ Jesus.

Romans 10:13-17

For whosoever shall call upon the name of the Lord shall be saved.

How then shall they call on him in whom they have not believed? and how shall they believe in him of whom they have not heard? and how shall they hear without a preacher?

And how shall they preach, except they be sent? as it is written, How beautiful are the feet of them that preach the gospel of peace, and bring glad tidings of good things!

But they have not all obeyed the gospel. For Esaias saith, Lord, who hath believed our report?

So then faith cometh by hearing, and hearing by the word of God.

Galatians 3:22-26

But the scripture hath concluded all under sin, that the promise by faith of Jesus Christ might be given to them that believe.

But before faith came, we were kept under the law, shut up unto the faith which should afterwards be revealed.

Wherefore the law was our schoolmaster to bring us unto Christ, that we might be justified by faith.

But after that faith is come, we are no longer under a schoolmaster.

For ye are all the children of God by faith in Christ Jesus.

THE SCHOOLMASTER/LAW:

Exodus 20:1-17

And God spake all these words, saying,

I am the Lord thy God, which have brought thee out of the land of Egypt, out of the house of bondage.

Thou shalt have no other gods before me.

Thou shalt not make unto thee any graven image, ...

Thou shalt not bow down thyself to them, ...

Thou shalt not take the name of the Lord thy God in vain; for the Lord will not hold him guiltless that taketh his name in vain. *(Leviticus 19:12 says "And ye shall not swear by my name falsely, neither shalt thou profane the name of thy God: I am the Lord.)*
Remember the sabbath day, to keep it holy....
Honour thy father and thy mother: that thy days may be long upon the land which the Lord thy God giveth thee.
Thou shalt not kill.
Thou shalt not commit adultery.
Thou shalt not steal.
Thou shalt not bear false witness against thy neighbour. *(Leviticus 19:11 says "You shall not steal, neither deal falsely, neither lie one to another."*
Thou shalt not covet thy neighbour's house, thou shalt not covet thy neighbour's wife, nor his manservant, nor his maidservant, nor his ox, nor his ass, nor any thing that is thy neighbour's.

Have you ever stolen anything? _____
Have you ever lied? _____
Have you ever coveted (longingly, wish for or desire) something of your neighbors? _____
Have you ever dishonored your father or mother ? _____
Have you ever profaned (to put to an improper, unworthy, irreverent or degrading use) God's name? _____

(This is just some of His law. To see some more of the commandments of God continue reading in Exodus and read Leviticus 19. If you broke the law in just one of His commandments then you are guilty of all: 'For whosoever shall keep the whole law, and yet offend in one point, he is guilty of all." James 2:10)

Romans 3:19-26
Now we know that what things soever the law saith, it saith to them who are under the law: that every mouth may be stopped, and all the world may become guilty before God.

Therefore by the deeds of the law there shall no flesh be justified in his sight: for by the law is the knowledge of sin.

But now the righteousness of God without the law is manifested, being witnessed by the law and the prophets;

Even the righteousness of God which is by faith of Jesus Christ unto all and upon all them that believe: for there is no difference:

For all have sinned, and come short of the glory of God;

Romans 6:23

For the wages of sin is death; but the gift of God is eternal life through Jesus Christ our Lord.

Romans 10:9-13

That if thou shalt confess with thy mouth the Lord Jesus, and shalt believe in thine heart that God hath raised him from the dead, thou shalt be saved.

For with the heart man believeth unto righteousness; and with the mouth confession is made unto salvation.

For the scripture saith, Whosoever believeth on him shall not be ashamed.

For there is no difference between the Jew and the Greek: for the same Lord over all is rich unto all that call upon him.

For whosoever shall call upon the name of the Lord shall be saved.

1 Peter 2:24

Who his own self bare our sins in his own body on the tree, that we, being dead to sins, should live unto righteousness: by whose stripes ye were healed.

Hebrews 9:26-28

For then must he often have suffered since the foundation of the world: but now once in the end of the world hath he appeared to put away sin by the sacrifice of himself.

And as it is appointed unto men once to die, but after this the judgment:
So Christ was once offered to bear the sins of many; and unto them that look for him shall he appear the second time without sin unto salvation.

1 Tim 1:15
This is a faithful saying, and worthy of all acceptation, that Christ Jesus came into the world to save sinners; of whom I am chief.

Romans 5:8
But God commendeth his love toward us, in that, while we were yet sinners, Christ died for us.

John 3:16-18
For God so loved the world, that he gave his only begotten Son, that whosoever believeth in him should not perish, but have everlasting life.
For God sent not his Son into the world to condemn the world; but that the world through him might be saved.
He that believeth on him is not condemned: but he that believeth not is condemned already, because he hath not believed in the name of the only begotten Son of God.

1 Corinthians 15:1-4
Moreover, brethren, I declare unto you the gospel which I preached unto you, which also ye have received, and wherein ye stand;
By which also ye are saved, if ye keep in memory what I preached unto you, unless ye have believed in vain.
For I delivered unto you first of all that which I also received, how that Christ died for our sins according to the scriptures;
And that he was buried, and that he rose again the third day according to the scriptures:

Luke 24:46-47
And said unto them, Thus it is written, and thus it behoved
Christ to suffer, and to rise from the dead the third day:
And that repentance and remission of sins should be preached
in his name among all nations, beginning at Jerusalem.

Acts 4:12
Neither is there salvation in any other: for there is none other
name under heaven given among men, whereby we must be
saved.

John 14:6
Jesus saith unto him, I am the way, the truth, and the life: no
man cometh unto the Father, but by me.

Matthew 7:13-14
Enter ye in at the strait gate: for wide is the gate, and broad is
the way, that leadeth to destruction, and many there be which
go in thereat:
Because strait is the gate, and narrow is the way, which leadeth
unto life, and few there be that find it.

IF YOU BELIEVE
THEN BE BAPTIZED

Acts 8:12
But when they believed Philip preaching the things concerning
the kingdom of God, and the name of Jesus Christ, they were
baptized, both men and women.

Acts 22:16
And now why tarriest thou? arise, and be baptized, and wash
away thy sins, calling on the name of the Lord.

58774905R00154

Made in the USA
Lexington, KY
16 December 2016